One subtle re ...
she was on fir ...
to do. Her feet ..... cooperating. They moved
her a step closer.

CJ's gray eyes turned thundercloud dark. Lifting
his hand, he cupped her cheek. "I have the feeling
you don't want me to go."

"I don't." Taking a shaky breath, she moved out of
reach. "But it's for the best."

He shoved both hands in the pockets of his jeans.
His chest heaved as his hot gaze met hers. "This
isn't going to work, Izzy. It's obvious you want me
as much as I want you. I can't see us accomplishing
much when we're both craving something you
claim we can't have."

"I underestimated the strength of our chemistry."

"No kidding."

"And my overactive hormones aren't helping. I
didn't consider that, either."

"Well, now you know. I must be picking up on
your hormonal overload because the minute I
come within ten feet, I want to kiss the living
daylights out of you. And damned if you don't look
like that would suit you just fine."

Baby-Daddy Cowboy

THE BUCKSKIN BROTHERHOOD

Vicki Lewis Thompson

Ocean Dance Press

BABY-DADDY COWBOY
© 2020 Vicki Lewis Thompson

ISBN: 978-1-946759-87-0

Ocean Dance Press LLC
PO Box 69901
Oro Valley, AZ 85737

Cover art by Sylvia Frost, The Book Brander

Visit the author's website at
VickiLewisThompson.com

Want more cowboys? Check out these other titles by
Vicki Lewis Thompson

The Buckskin Brotherhood
Sweet-Talking Cowboy
Big-Hearted Cowboy
Baby-Daddy Cowboy

The McGavin Brothers
A Cowboy's Strength
A Cowboy's Honor
A Cowboy's Return
A Cowboy's Heart
A Cowboy's Courage
A Cowboy's Christmas
A Cowboy's Kiss
A Cowboy's Luck
A Cowboy's Charm
A Cowboy's Challenge
A Cowboy's Baby
A Cowboy's Holiday
A Cowboy's Choice
A Cowboy's Worth
A Cowboy's Destiny
A Cowboy's Secret
A Cowboy's Homecoming

1

"It doesn't get any better'n this, Jake." CJ Andrews sliced up an onion and dumped it in a bowl before picking up a second one. "Beautiful summer day and your chuck-wagon stew for dinner. Thanks for making it."

"My pleasure." Cubed beef sizzled in the frying pan as Jake browned the meat.

"I was afraid you'd give up on the Friday night tradition." Soon after Matt and Lucy's wedding two months ago, Jake and Millie had paired up, further reducing the number of single men in the Buckskin Brotherhood.

"I was tempted to ditch you guys." Jake grinned. "But I hate to see grown men cry."

"I would've cried for sure. I wait all week for this night."

"CJ, you seriously need to get a life."

"Don't I know it, bro." He quartered the potatoes. "But for now, having you and Matt join the Brotherhood for dinner once a week is the highlight of my existence. When we're all sitting around the table, it's like you two never left."

Jake laughed. "You see us every blessed day."

"You know what I mean."

"Yeah, I do. I need our Friday night routine as much as anyone. Millie likes it, too. Gives her a chance to hang out with Kate and Lucy."

CJ's phone chimed. "See, I have a life. People call me." He grabbed a towel and quickly dried his hands before tugging his phone from his pocket. "Probably Nick wanting to know if the stew's ready." He glanced at the screen and sucked in air.

"CJ?" Jake peered at him. "You okay?"

"It's Isabel." The one woman he'd never expected to hear from again. "'Scuse me." He tapped the screen, put the phone to his ear and managed a jaunty greeting.

"Hey, CJ." She sounded weird. Strained. Not like the bubbly Isabel Ricchetti who'd been one of the bridesmaids for Matt and Lucy's wedding.

The last night of her stay, she'd invited him to share her bed and he'd accepted. One night of carefree sex. That was all he'd counted on and all she'd been willing to give.

"What's wrong, Iz?"

"I'm pregnant."

He gripped the phone as he fought for breath. "But... we used—"

"I know."

"Are you sure?"

"Just got back from the doctor."

He gulped. *Think, man. Say something.* "I want to see you."

She let out a gusty sigh. "I was hoping you'd suggest that."

He closed his eyes. He'd said the right thing. "We'll talk, figure this out." He dragged in a breath. "I'll come there." A last-minute ticket to Seattle would be pricey. Didn't matter.

"No, let me come to you. I have frequent flier miles. And I'd like to talk with Lucy, too."

"You've told her?"

"Not yet. I wanted to call you first. She'll be next. Then my... folks." Her voice quivered.

"Izzy, it'll be okay. We'll handle this together."

She sniffed. "You're a kind man, CJ. I knew that, but I... anyway, I'd better hang up before I get weepy. I'll text you when I have a ticket. Bye." The line went dead.

He stared at the phone. A baby. His baby. His gut clenched.

"I got the gist of that." Jake's voice penetrated the fog. "Sounds like she's pregnant."

CJ nodded, opened his mouth to comment and closed it again. He must have used all his words while talking with Isabel.

"Go grab yourself a cold one. I'll finish this up."

"No, I can—"

"Forget it. You'll slice off your pinky. You need a bottle of hard cider and you need it now. Get one and have a seat at the table. Once the stew's in the pot, I'll join you." He paused. "Don't worry, bro. You've got this."

"Not even close."

"Get your cider."

"Okay." He tucked his phone in his pocket, headed for the fridge and opened the door. Jake was right about the cider. Wrapping his hand around a chilled bottle was a familiar sensation that steadied him. He twisted off the cap and took a long swallow of the tangy brew. Better.

"Stew done yet?" Nick's voice boomed out as he came through the front door of the bunkhouse. "I'm starving."

Another dose of normal. Nick ate like a horse and could probably bench-press one. The guy lifted weights a *lot.*

"You're always starving!" Jake called back. "Stew will be ready when it's ready."

"What kind of answer is—" Nick broke off as he walked into the kitchen. "Whoa, CJ. Did somebody die?"

"Just the opposite." CJ lifted his bottle in salute. "In seven months, somebody will be born."

"Who?"

"My kid."

Nick's eyes widened. "No shit." He nudged back his hat. "Isabel?"

"Yep." CJ took another fortifying gulp of his cider.

"Anything I can do?"

"What do you know about pregnant ladies?"

"They have weird food cravings. Gertie at the sandwich shop told me that."

Jake turned from the stove. "What a shock that your intel concerns food. Hey, since you're here, how about washing up and then chopping some cabbage for coleslaw?"

"Sure, but CJ usually—"

"CJ's not allowed to risk dismembering himself right now."

"Oh. Got it." Nick rolled back his sleeves and cleaned up at the sink. "I must say I'm surprised at this turn of events, CJ. I pegged you as a condom-wearing man."

"I am. I did. Purchased that weekend."

"Then maybe you slipped up on the withdraw." Nick dried his hands and picked up the head of cabbage on the counter. "Get a little careless on that maneuver and—"

"I was careful, and this discussion is over. Isabel is pregnant and we're not going to dissect why and how."

"Understood." Nick glanced over at him as he picked up a large knife. "Didn't mean to intrude. In your shoes, I wouldn't want that, either." Focusing on the cutting board, he began whacking at the head of cabbage. "Hey, this is more fun than I expected!"

"Easy, Nick." Jake laid a hand on his arm. "Chop, don't pulverize."

"Oh. Then this is good enough?"

"Perfect." Jake rescued the mangled remains of the cabbage. "Appreciate the help."

"Anytime. I didn't realize cooking was so physically rewarding. I need to do more of it." He headed for the fridge. "Cider, Jake?"

"Sure. I'll be done here in a minute."

"CJ?"

"Thanks, but I'm still working on this one." Much as he'd love to get toasted, he needed all his brain cells for this crisis.

Nick brought two bottles to the table and twisted the cap off one. Pulling out a chair, he spun it around and straddled it. "What's the plan, bro? How can we help?"

"Don't know, yet." He'd never been so glad to be a part of the Brotherhood. No matter what, they'd have his back. "Isabel's coming here so we can talk face-to-face."

"That's good. When?"

"As soon as she can book a flight. Which reminds me. I need to call Henri and see what she has in the way of cabins."

Jake turned from the stove. "Better do that now. We're pretty full."

"Right." CJ took out his phone to call Henri Fox, the woman who'd started out as his boss ten years ago and had gradually become the mother figure who'd seen him through some tough times. This was shaping up to be another one.

Nick picked up his cider. "Gonna tell her why Isabel's coming?"

"Not on the phone." He sat up straighter and put the phone to his ear. "Hi, Henri. It's me."

"How're you doing, son?"

"I'm okay. Listen, Isabel's coming for a visit. Do you have a cabin available?"

"Lucy called five minutes ago. I've already reserved a one-bedroom. Last one we had."

"Thank you."

"Lucy said Isabel's in the family way."

He gulped. "Henri, I swear that I—"

"You don't have to say a word. My boys aren't careless about such things. Stuff happens.

You'll be fine, CJ. Isabel and the baby will be, too. It'll work out."

"Yes, ma'am." He wasn't nearly that confident, but he appreciated the sentiment. "I'll cover the cabin rental. You can take it out of my paycheck."

"I won't be doing that."

"But it's my—"

"Not exactly. You aren't the only one affected by this change in circumstances."

"What do you mean?"

"I'm claiming grandmother rights to this child."

He blinked. "I did *not* see that coming."

"I never wanted to put pressure on any of you, but I've been hoping for babies eventually. Seth and Zoe gave me a taste when they brought little Hamish up for the wedding. Isabel's part of the family, now. I don't charge family members rent."

His throat tightened. "Thank you."

"Give yourself time, CJ. I predict before too long you'll start getting excited about this news."

"Yes, ma'am." Nope. He'd never been this terrified, not even when he'd been lost in a blizzard with no cell phone.

"Do I have your permission to tell the Babes?" Her closest friends had formed a barrel-racing group called Babes on Buckskins. She made it sound like they'd be thrilled, too.

"Uh... I guess so."

"Great. Then I'll let you get on with whatever you were doing."

"You mean quietly freaking out?"

She chuckled. "Like I said, give yourself time. Let me know when you have Isabel's ETA. 'Bye, son."

"'Bye, Henri." He disconnected and checked the phone for a text. Nothing yet. He laid it on the table where he could see the screen.

Jake came over and took a seat. "She already knew, didn't she?"

He nodded. "Isabel called Lucy after talking to me. Lucy contacted Henri." He glanced at Jake and Nick. "She's claiming grandmother rights and wants to tell the Babes."

Both guys smiled.

"See?" Jake raised his bottle in a salute. "Somebody thinks this is good news."

Nick laughed. "She'll make a helluva granny."

"Wish I could say the same about my chances of being a decent father."

Nick's gaze was sympathetic. "We'll all be here for you, bro."

"I appreciate the moral support. But the only one with actual experience in fatherhood isn't available."

"Sure he is." Nick held up his phone. "We can have a virtual Seth in no time."

"A virtual Seth. That's funny."

"It *is* funny. People don't look quite right in those video chats." Nick shrugged. "But it's still better than not seeing him at all."

"We can hold off on that. This baby is seven months away." He swallowed. "And likely will be born in Seattle. I probably won't get much chance to—"

"Whoa, there, partner," Jake said. "Back up the negativity bus. You don't know how much contact you'll have with the little tyke. Point of fact, you don't know *anything*."

"I know Isabel's pregnant with our baby. And I also know I'm not ready for fatherhood."

"Understandable reaction," Nick said. "Most guys would feel as if they—"

"I'm serious. I have no clue how a dad is supposed to behave. I never knew mine. Sure, I had Charley. We all did, but we were practically grown when he and Henri took us on. It's not the same as being responsible for a tiny, vulnerable human."

"I suppose not." Nick picked at the label on his bottle. "I didn't know my dad, either." He glanced up. "He cut out before I was born."

"I wish mine had." Jake took a gulp of his cider.

"That's what I'm saying, Jake. If any of us had been lucky enough to have a wonderful, supportive dad, we wouldn't have ended up at the Buckskin Ranch."

Jake's gaze was steady. "And that's our reward for being survivors. We've learned to roll with the punches. Like I said, you've got this."

2

CJ. Isabel's breath caught. He hadn't seen her yet, which gave her a moment to admire the father of her unborn child. He stood straight and tall, his broad shoulders thrust back, his hat clutched in one hand, his sleeves rolled to his elbows in deference to the summer heat. He scanned the crowd, his brow furrowed in concentration. The overhead lights added a glow to his sun-streaked hair. Almost a halo.

But CJ Andrews was no angel. He'd proven that several times over during their lusty night together. One glimpse of him and her body tightened, eager for more of the same. But that wasn't her goal on this trip. Making love to him would only complicate an already dicey situation.

When he spotted her, he replaced his frown with a wide smile and started forward. Evidently her arrival made him happy, even under difficult circumstances. Thank God for that.

They'd liked each other from the moment they'd met. She wanted to maintain that positive vibe as they worked out the details of long-distance co-parenting. Hooking the strap of her small carryon over her shoulder, she went to meet him.

His ground-eating strides dissolved the space between them and he drew her into his arms without the slightest hesitation. "You look great."

"Thanks. You, too." She rested her hands on his muscled chest and looked up. The expression in his warm gray eyes tugged on her heart, just like the last time they'd stood in this terminal saying goodbye. "I've missed you." Where had that come from?

"I've missed you, too." Lowering his head, he brushed his lips over hers before pulling back to gaze at her. "Told myself I didn't."

"Same here." She took a shaky breath and resisted the urge to nestle closer to his warm body. "I'm so glad to see you, but... I've decided we'll be better off if we... if we don't make love while I'm here."

He blinked. "Really? Is it bad for the baby?"

"No. But it could be bad for us."

He gave her a crooked grin. "That's not how I remember it."

Her skin tingled as a flush spread from head to toe. "Not bad in that sense. Bad for our future."

"How so?"

"In the long run, this situation will work out better if we're just friends."

His gaze searched hers. "If that's what you believe is best." He swallowed. "But I won't lie. I still want you. That hasn't changed."

The air between them sizzled and popped as the heat in his eyes turned her insides to molten lava. Two months ago, she'd tossed aside her better judgment because of that look. She'd had the freedom to do that.

Resisting him wouldn't be easy. "Not for me, either, but more is on the line this time, and I can't think clearly when I'm... when we're involved in—"

"Let's table this discussion." He gave her a quick hug and let her go. "We'll fetch your luggage and head to the ranch. I have a million questions about the baby."

She abandoned the topic of sex with relief. Once they were on the road, he immediately began asking questions about the baby's current stage of development and how pregnancy was affecting her. She was up on all of it. She'd had a long chat with her doctor and her sister Naomi had gathered a ton of info online.

"No morning sickness, then?"

"Not so far, thank goodness. My mom didn't have it with me or Naomi, so maybe I'll dodge that bullet. Mom said the women in her family tend to take childbirth in stride."

"That's lucky." He drove with easy confidence.

He made love with easy confidence, too. She'd never been with someone who was the perfect combo of relaxed and intense. She needed to derail that train of thought ASAP or the question about sex or no sex would be moot. She concentrated on the spectacular mountain scenery out the window instead of the gorgeous cowboy beside her.

"I never asked you, but is Ricchetti Italian?"

"Portuguese."

"Portuguese? Now that's interesting. What about your mom?"

"She also has Portuguese ancestors by a weird coincidence."

"Everybody says the baby will take after you instead of me because dark eyes and hair are dominant over light hair and eyes."

"It's not a done deal. My family tends toward dark hair and brown eyes, but there could be a throwback to a distant ancestor. I could have a towhead."

"*We* could have a towhead."

"Yes, sorry. I didn't mean to—"

"I want to be part of this, but I have to warn you I'm the weak link. I'll need parenting classes and tons of coaching. I know zilch about babies."

A slow ache built in her chest. Clearly this was an area in which he didn't feel confident. His plans for educating himself were sweet, but might be unnecessary. "Considering the baby and I will be more than six hundred miles away, you might not need to spend too much time on—"

"I'll make the drive."

"CJ, it's a ten-hour trip."

"I'm aware. I figured it out. I can't afford to fly on a regular basis, so I'll schedule three days off whenever possible."

"That sounds like tough duty, twenty hours of driving for a very short stay."

"Not as tough as you'll have it on a regular basis. I've talked with Sarah at Gertie's Sandwich Shop. She had a baby seven weeks ago, but her mom's in charge of the shop, so Sarah doesn't have full responsibility for the operation like you do. I don't know how you'll run Cup of Cheer and take care of a newborn."

"I'll have seven months to figure it out."

"Who did you put in charge for this week?"

"My little sister. When I took time off for the wedding, I made sure my veteran staff members would be there, but this was last minute. Two of my key people are on vacation and I hate to dump full responsibility on her for a week, but..."

"Should be okay."

"Hope so. I considered making it a three-day trip, but Naomi and my folks talked me into taking a full week. They don't think we should rush this discussion."

"I like them already."

"They like you already, especially after I told them how you responded to my phone call."

"How do they feel about the baby?"

"Like you, they're worried about how I'll manage the coffee shop and a baby. But they're excited about having a grandchild."

"Henri's excited about that, too."

"Your boss? Are you related to her?"

"Not officially. None of us are, but we're all her boys, anyway. She's... she's hoping you'll bring the baby for visits. She wants to do the grandmother thing."

"I will bring the baby as often as I can manage. You shouldn't have to do all the traveling. It's just that I—"

"You have a business to run and I don't. I'll make the drive. I don't want you to feel like you're alone in this."

A lump lodged in her throat. "Thanks, CJ."

"You're welcome."

"I should probably find out what that stands for."

"What?"

"CJ. When I fill out this child's birth certificate, I don't want to put down initials for the father's name. I'm assuming they stand for something."

He grinned. "They do."

"Why is that funny?"

"Allow me to introduce myself. I'm Cornelius Jasper Andrews."

She stared at him. "You're kidding."

"Not kidding. And I challenge you to find a decent nickname somewhere in that combo. Other than CJ."

"Neil?"

He glanced at her. "Do I look like a Neil to you?"

"Definitely not. CJ sounds like a cowboy."

He laughed. "I thought so, too, and here I am."

"Did you ever go by Cornelius?"

"The first five years of my life. Then I started school and figured out real quick that wasn't going to fly. I've been CJ ever since."

"I've never met a Cornelius."

"Me, either. When my mother was in high school she did a report on Cornelius Vanderbilt. She said naming me after him might bring me good luck. Maybe I'd be destined for fame and fortune, too."

"Then I'm confused about Jasper. She could have given you Vanderbilt as a middle name to add even more fairy dust."

"I figure Jasper was my father's name, but she said it wasn't. She was barely seventeen when I was born. My best guess is that my dad's family had money and they bought her off. She refused to tell me who my dad was, but she got monthly checks from a lawyer's office. She wouldn't reveal the source of those, either."

"Are you in touch with her?"

"She died in a car accident when I was sixteen."

"Oh, dear. Were you in the car?"

"No. She was on her way to work."

"That's sad. Both of you were so young."

"Yeah. I didn't take it well. I hated the idea of foster care, which is where I was likely headed, so I left town. Drifted from place to place working odd jobs for almost three years. Then Charley hired me."

"Henri's late husband?"

"Yep. I only had a father figure for six years, but I doubt I could have picked a better one if I'd tried."

"He must have been a wonderful guy. When Lucy wasn't raving about how adorable Matt was, she'd go on about Henri and Charley. Her family vacations to the Buckskin Ranch were her favorite thing."

"Henri and Charley doted on her, too." He paused. "Did Lucy ever mention me?"

"Oh, yeah, she talked about all the guys. Jake, the tease, Nick, the bottomless pit, Leo, the beautiful one, Rafe, the gentle giant. Of course, Matt was the principal focus of her cowboy fantasies."

"Sounds like she had a designation for each of us."

"She did."

"You neglected to mention mine."

"The sweet one who sort of played guitar."

"Ugh."

"Don't worry. She told me later you'd become really good at it."

"I'm fine with the mediocre musician label. It's *the sweet one* that makes me cringe."

"Why do men hate being called sweet? It's a compliment."

"It's only one notch above *nice,* which is the kiss of death for getting dates. I'm surprised you had anything to do with me if she told you I was *sweet.*"

"It so happens I like that in a man."

"Lucky me."

She hesitated. "Do you mean that?"

"Absolutely." He looked over at her in surprise. "Did you think I was being sarcastic?"

"Well, people do say *lucky me* when referring to *bad* luck, and if I hadn't invited you to spend the night, you wouldn't be facing—"

"If you hadn't invited me to spend the night, I would have missed out on one of the peak experiences of my life."

Her breath stalled. "That's how you think of it?"

"Yes, ma'am." He returned his attention to the road. "I know it's landed us in a sticky situation, but I wouldn't change anything."

She slowly released air from her lungs, and the tension that had plagued her since she'd made her phone call on Friday flowed out with it. "Neither would I."

3

During the one-hour drive from Great Falls International, CJ had revealed more about his history than he'd shared with anyone, including the Brotherhood. But Isabel was carrying their child. She deserved to know everything he could tell her.

He slowed as they approached Apple Grove. An apple-shaped billboard announced the town's slogan—*Johnny Appleseed's Success Story!* The road led to the square, but he planned to hang a right before they got there and take the two-lane out to the ranch.

He glanced at her. "Need anything from town before we head out?"

"A bathroom. Mom warned me I'd have to go a lot and I didn't believe her, so I drank plenty of water on the plane like I usually do to stay hydrated. And now...I believe my mom."

"No worries. Sarah told me about that, too. We can head to the sandwich shop and grab a snack, too, if you're hungry."

"That's perfect. It's called Gertie's Sandwich Shop, right?"

"Yes, ma'am."

"Who is Gertie? Is she still around?"

"The original Gertie has passed. She left the sandwich shop to Sarah's grandmother, who decided to use the name Gertie whenever she was in the shop. Her daughter, Sarah's mom, followed suit and it became a tradition. Sarah is a fourth-generation Gertie." He spotted a diagonal parking space right in front.

"That's good marketing. Did Sarah have a girl?"

"She did. If the tradition continues, Sarah will inherit the business and her daughter will follow in her footsteps." Pots of geraniums sat outside and two small umbrella tables, each with a couple of chairs, created a mini sidewalk cafe. Lunchtime was over and no one was taking advantage of the ambiance.

"That's cool, that they've kept the shop in the family that long. Speaking of passing things on, I need to update my will."

"There's a jolly subject."

"Wills are necessary, though. Do you have a will?"

"No, ma'am." He parked the truck and shut off the engine.

"You should probably get one."

"But I don't have any assets to—"

"Gotta go. See you in there." She was out of the truck in a flash and flung the door closed.

He hopped down and followed her, but she was through the glass front door of Gertie's before he had a chance to open it for her. Clearly he'd miscalculated the urgency of the situation. Next time he'd know better.

When he walked in, she was nowhere to be seen. A young couple he didn't recognize, likely tourists, were having a late lunch in the far corner by the front window, but otherwise, the place was deserted.

Sarah stood behind the counter and gave him a smile. She'd cut her blond hair short since having the baby. "I take it that was Isabel who zipped into the restroom?"

"Yes, ma'am."

"I thought I recognized her from the last time she was in town. How's she doing?"

"Good, I think. No morning sickness so far. She just needed a bathroom real quick."

"It comes with the territory. You folks want something to eat?"

"Probably just a snack. How's little Amy?"

"Fine. She's asleep in the kitchen."

"You brought her?"

"Best option when John's at work and I need to be here. Mom loves having Amy around. She just went back to *check on her.*" She made air quotes. "We have a baby monitor so there's no need, but Mom likes watching her granddaughter sleep. It's cute how she dotes on that little girl."

"I wonder if Isabel has thought of taking the baby to work with her."

"Why not? You said she owns the coffee shop. She—ah, here she comes. Hi, Isabel! I made an educated guess that's who you were."

Isabel walked over to the counter. "And you're Sarah, aka Gertie?"

"Most days I'm Sarah-slash-Gertie. But sometimes I prefer to think of myself as Queen

Esmeralda, living in a castle and waited on by handmaidens."

Isabel laughed. "I'll might need to steal that fantasy once the baby's born. CJ said you've talked to him about pregnancy and childbirth."

"I have, although everybody's different. He mentioned you've been spared morning sickness. That's a win."

"So I hear. Considering that, I can't complain about the bathroom issue."

"Any food cravings?"

"Right now, anything salty, preferably a carb."

"How does a serving of wedge-cut fries sound?"

"Orgasmic."

CJ blinked. Had she really said that? After their recent discussion, which had him thinking he'd be taking a lot of cold showers? He glanced at her and she had the good grace to blush and look away.

Sarah turned to him. "What'll you have?"

"The same, thanks." Maybe warm fries could be a substitute for hot sex. He doubted it, but he might have to make do. "Izzy, want to sit outside?"

"Love to."

"Good choice, guys. It's gorgeous out there." She glanced at Isabel. "Something to drink?"

"Apple cider, please. I'll have to lay off the hard version but the regular is delicious, too."

"I'll have one, as well." CJ took money from his wallet and added a tip to the amount showing on the cash register. "Thanks, Sarah."

"You bet." She handed him a receipt. "Go soak up some sunshine. I'll bring your order out in a few minutes." She started toward the kitchen. "Aha! I hear Amy."

Isabel glanced in that direction as muted wails punctuated by jerky hiccups filtered through the swinging kitchen door. "Your daughter?"

She nodded. "My mom's watching her. Naptime must be over."

"I would love to see her."

"I'll bring her out after she's fed and changed. My Mom will be taking care of your order." She pushed through the swinging door to the kitchen.

"Sarah's just given me an idea."

"I thought she might."

"Naomi's looking forward to this baby, so she'd probably like the idea of bringing him or her to work."

"Beats getting a sitter." He gestured toward the door. "Let's go claim our table."

She laughed. "Before someone else does?" She started toward the front of the shop, which was empty now that the young couple had left. "Somehow I expected Apple Grove to be bustling now that the snow's gone."

"The tourists are here, but they're out and about this time of day." He followed her. "We tend to get active folks. They're out riding, or they've gone to Glacier for the day, or they're exploring the hiking trails in this area. The Choosy Moose will be jumping tonight, which usually isn't true on a Monday in the winter."

"I'd love to go to the Moose while I'm here, even if I can't have hard cider."

"Then plan on it." This time he managed to get the door for her. "I'm sure the gang will be up for a Choosy Moose evening."

"Hope so." She pointed to the table closest to the door. "Let's take this one."

He pulled out a chair for her. "For the staff's convenience?"

"Yeah, I do it automatically, now. In this case, it doesn't matter so much, but why not save them a few steps?" She glanced over her shoulder as he helped her into her chair. "Thank you."

"You're welcome." He took a seat across from her.

"Lucy told me the Buckskin cowboys are big on manners, but until I came to the wedding, I thought she was exaggerating."

"Henri and Charley worked on us." The canvas chair was on the small side, but the view across the table was primo. Isabel's dark hair fell in shiny waves around her slender shoulders and her deep-set brown eyes held that special gleam that said she was happy to be with him. He could look at Isabel all day. And all night, for that matter.

"Henri and Charley gave you instructions on how to behave?"

"Sometimes. Mostly they set an example and expected us to follow it. Seth had manners from the get-go because he was raised on the Buckskin. The rest of us had some rough edges. Henri and Charley sanded them off."

"I can't imagine you with rough edges. Did your mom let you get away with stuff?"

"All the time."

"She did?"

"You have to remember she was still in high school when she had me. She made a stab at being an adult, but she was more of a buddy than a mom. I asked for a guitar and she got me one. Sold some collectible dolls she'd been given as a kid."

"She sounds very loving."

"Loving, yes, but she was no disciplinarian. I wasn't used to following rules, which is why I lit out to escape living with foster parents. I knew they'd make me toe the line."

"Why did you agree to follow rules at the Buckskin?"

"I fell in love with the place. And the people. Henri and Charley taught me that being a cowboy involved more than riding and roping skills. They demanded a respectful attitude, kindness to those less fortunate and courage in the face of adversity."

Her expression softened. "That's you all over. You showed all those things when I called you on Friday."

He grinned. "I was quaking in my boots."

"Me, too. Except I wasn't wearing boots."

"Do you have any?"

"Girly ones with four-inch heels, but that day I had on flats."

"You don't have riding boots?"

"I've never been on a horse."

"What?"

The gleam of amusement was back. "Not everyone makes that a priority, you know."

"Lucy didn't take you when you were here for the wedding?"

"We didn't have time. She promised we'd go out this visit."

"Is it safe for the baby?"

"So I've been told. Besides, I'm a beginner. We'll only be moseying down the trail."

"I'd like to take you out, too, then."

"I don't know about that, CJ." She was smiling, though, which usually didn't signal a rejection. "I'm not sure I could handle it."

"Why? It would be exactly like going with Lucy. We'd meander down the trail at a snail's pace."

"It would be nothing like going with Lucy. I've never seen you ride a horse, but I'm sure you're very good at it."

"I am, which means I'll keep you safe. And I'm a decent riding coach, too."

"I have no doubt, but the thing is, I'll have trouble keeping my hands to myself this week as it is. If I'm confronted with you in full cowboy mode astride a gallant steed, I might not be able to control myself."

At last, an opening. "We need to talk about that. You just admitted you want me as much as ever. Why do we have to lock it down this week? Why can't we—"

"Because now we're linked together by this child, and we will be for the rest of our lives. But we never intended to build a life together."

His chest tightened. "Did you meet someone? Is that what this is all about?"

"No, I didn't. But I will someday, and when I do, I want to feel…"

"Free?" Her point was logical. And he hated it.

"Yes."

He couldn't argue with that. Time to wave the white flag, damn it. He heaved a sigh. "Okay."

"I want you to feel free, too. I can't be your life partner and you deserve to find a woman who can be."

He gazed at her in helpless frustration. He hadn't felt free since their night together in April. Dating held no appeal. The woman he wanted was sitting across from him.

This was going to be one hell of a week.

<u>4</u>

Isabel had expected to struggle with this issue but she'd counted on CJ to embrace the concept once she'd explained it. Instead he sat there with his arms crossed over his broad chest and a scowl on his handsome face.

Well, he had mentioned that for the first sixteen years of his life he'd mostly gotten his way. She ducked her head, because it wouldn't do for him to catch her smiling at his belligerent pose.

He was an intelligent guy, so eventually he'd figure out he'd be better off accepting this short-term sacrifice for a long-term gain—a future in which they co-parented as friends, not lovers. In that scenario, they could happily dance at each other's wedding when the time came.

CJ would likely find someone before she did. He'd admitted back in April that he was looking for a commitment. Because of that, she hadn't intended to invite him into her bed. Then he'd hinted that he'd prefer one night to having nothing. Game over.

Sarah's mom brought out their fries, their cider and a bottle of catsup. After introducing herself to Isabel and chatting with them for a moment, she went back inside to help Sarah with Amy.

"Yum." Isabel created a little pool of catsup on her plate, dipped a fry in the sauce and finished it in two bites. "Exactly what I needed."

"Is it *orgasmic*?"

"A slip of the tongue on my part. I apologize."

"A Freudian slip?" He'd crossed his arms over his chest again.

"Possibly." She met his hot gaze. "It would help if you'd stop looking at me like that." She broke eye contact and picked up another fry.

"How am I looking at you?"

"You know perfectly well." She ate the fry and glanced at him. "It's obvious what you're thinking."

"And you're not?" Uncrossing his arms, he reached for his bottle of cider and took a slow sip, drawing her attention to his mouth.

On purpose? "Now I am."

He put down the bottle and leaned his muscled forearms on the table. "Because you can't help it any more than I can. I've considered what you said, and it makes sense, but—"

"Let me guess. You want to start that program after I leave next weekend."

"What's wrong with that?" He dumped catsup over all his fries and started eating.

He might regret telling her about his indulgent mother. She had his number, now. "Have you dated since I left in April?"

She'd caught him with his mouth full. He shook his head and kept chewing.

"Why?"

He finished chewing and swallowed. "Didn't feel like it."

"But you told me you were tired of the single life, especially after seeing how well a steady relationship is working for your buddies."

"Yes, ma'am, that's a fact."

"I've been to the Choosy Moose. It looks like a great place to meet someone."

"None of them compare to you."

Even though that thrilled her, she had to pursue this discussion to its conclusion. "And there's the problem. I'm flattered, but if that's how you feel after you've spent one night with me, what will happen after six?"

"You won't be able to wipe the smile off my face. Or yours."

"CJ! I'm trying to be serious."

"So am I. If we follow your plan, we'll be in a constant state of frustration." He flashed her a triumphant glance. "*That* can't be good for the baby."

"I don't know. I haven't researched it."

"You don't have to. Too much of anything is bad. I may not have a high-school diploma, but I read. Moderation is the healthy way to go."

"In my experience, you don't practice moderation in bed."

"Because I had to cram everything into one night. Give me six and I'll practice moderation like you wouldn't believe."

That coaxed a grin out of her. "Somehow I doubt that."

"Give me a chance to prove it."

His comments stirred her up more than she cared to admit. Munching on her fries, she attempted a nonchalant attitude as she studied him. "You're very good at this."

"What?"

"Getting your way."

His expression brightened. "Then you agree that we can—"

"I didn't say that. I'm still right. You need to get over me so you can find someone else. Having more sex this week is going in the wrong direction."

"You never know. Maybe we'll be sick to death of each other by Sunday morning." He took a long pull on his cider.

"We won't and you know it."

'Yeah, I do." He sighed. "It was one argument I hadn't tried so I threw it out there."

"And I'm sticking to my guns. I can handle a few days of sexual frustration and I can't believe it would impact our baby. But if I let our relationship derail your search for happiness, that will have far-reaching consequences."

"What if I promise to start dating the day after you leave? I'll go to the Moose more often. I'll sign up for one of those dating apps. More than one, even. I'll—"

"After we've spent every night together for the entire week? You're not that shallow. If you were, you'd be involved with someone new by now."

He took a deep breath. "In case you can't tell, I'm scraping the bottom of my barrel of arguments."

"Then let me give you one of mine. Because you're a gentleman and a cowboy, I suspect this is the one I should have used all along."

"I'll bet I don't want to hear it."

"Probably not, but you should." She paused. "I also need to get over you."

His gaze locked with hers. Resignation clouded the gray depths of his eyes. "Yes, ma'am. That does the trick."

The dejection in his expression tore her to pieces. What to say? This was the right move, so why did it make her heart hurt?

Sarah provided a welcome distraction when she nudged open the door and came out with Amy in her arms. Isabel stood and CJ followed her lead.

"You guys don't have to get up!" Sarah laughed. "Amy's not royalty."

"Sure she is," Isabel said. "If you're Queen Esmeralda, she must be a princess."

"My mom would agree with you. Since Amy's in an excellent mood right now, would you like to hold her?"

"I'd love to." Isabel gathered her courage and took the tiny girl from Sarah. She wasn't used to babies, hadn't held many. Most of her friends were unmarried and none had become parents. But she would be one, soon, and she wanted to be prepared.

She mimicked the way Sarah had cradled the infant—Amy's head resting in the crook of her mother's elbow and her tiny body supported by her mother's arms. The little girl smelled like lilacs. "Did you give her a bath?"

"A quick one. I wanted her to be at her best when she met you guys."

"She smells delicious."

"It's a local woman who makes soap. It's very gentle. Even if it gets in her eyes, it won't burn."

"I should take some home with me." Isabel gazed into wide eyes that were the color of denim. "Will her eyes stay that color?"

"They'll probably be blue since John and I both have blue eyes, but they could turn green. It'll be fun to watch."

"She's beautiful, Sarah." Amy's wispy hair was so pale it was almost white. Her pink rosebud of a mouth opened as she looked up at Isabel. Her lips curved.

Isabel was entranced. "Is that a smile?"

"I tell myself it is, but Mom says it's only gas at this age."

"I'm going to believe she's smiling at me."

"So do I. To heck with science."

"I don't know how you get any work done with this cutie-pie around."

"I was worried about that, but she sleeps a lot. That helps. And logic kicks in. If I spend all my time ogling the baby, I won't be an efficient employee and my paycheck will be in jeopardy. My little family needs that paycheck."

"I'll keep that in mind when it's my turn to be both mommy and boss-lady." She glanced at Sarah. "Could we meet sometime this week so I can pick your brain about how to handle a job and a newborn?"

"Absolutely. Give me your number before you leave and we'll set something up." Sarah looked over Isabel's shoulder. "CJ? Want to hold Amy?"

"I sure do. Like I told Izzy, babies aren't my strong suit. Any instruction or practice I can get, I'm going for it. "

"That's a great attitude. John felt the same and now he's a hands-on dad—changes diapers, rocks her to sleep and brings her in to me for the two a.m. feedings."

"That's great." Isabel envied Sarah that, but no point in wishing for something she couldn't have. She turned to CJ and stepped closer. "She's all yours."

His chest heaved and he frowned in concentration as he lifted Amy gently and tucked her into the crook of his elbow. She looked much smaller cradled in his muscled arms.

He stared at her in silence for a moment. "Hey, Amy," he murmured. "How's it going, girl?"

The baby gazed at him intently. Then she gurgled and waved her fists.

"That good, huh?" His expression slowly relaxed. "Well, sweetie, it only gets better from here. You're gonna love growing up in this town."

"That's the truth," Sarah said. "I know I did, and it hasn't changed much since I was a kid."

"Hear that, Amy?" CJ smiled. "You've got it made." Then he leaned down and kissed her forehead. "Nice meeting you. We'll have to do this again sometime." Moving toward Sarah, he handed the baby over in one smooth motion. "Thanks for letting me hold her. It was fun."

Sarah chuckled. "I could tell. You don't have to worry about practicing, CJ. You're a natural." She glanced at Isabel. "Don't you think so?"

She cleared the tightness from her throat. "Absolutely." After a moment of uncertainty, he'd settled right in. If he could connect so easily with someone else's baby, he would go bananas over his own.

She hadn't figured on that, either.

5

"That was way easier than I expected it to be." CJ backed out of the parking space in front of Gertie's, drove around the square and pointed the truck toward home. "Amy's a cool little kid."

"You're the cool one." Isabel glanced over at him. "Are you sure you've never held a baby?"

"Never. When I first got my hands on her, I was worried that I'd do it wrong. But then I looked at that cute face and those big blue eyes and talking to her just felt natural. I think she liked that."

"I think she did." Isabel continued to focus on him, like he was a riddle she had to solve. "After seeing you with Amy, I have a hunch you'll want to spend a lot of time with our baby after he or she is born."

"As much as I can manage. Do you know if we'll have a boy or a girl?"

"It's too early to tell."

"Makes sense. When will the doc be able to tell?"

"Another six or eight weeks."

"You'll let me know?"

"Are you saying you want to find out in advance?"

"Absolutely. Don't you?"

"I'd like to have it be a surprise. But you get a vote."

"Why wouldn't you want to know?"

"I'd rather wait and find out on the big day. But since we won't be together for my next appointment, my doctor could call and tell you after I leave."

He shook his head. "That's starting off on the wrong foot. Going forward, we should agree as much as possible. Besides, I don't want to know something you don't. I could mess that up by accidentally saying it."

"That brings up something else. How do you want to communicate during the next seven months?"

"Phone, I guess."

"You don't do email?"

"No need for it. But if that's what you like, I could get an account."

"That's not necessary. The phone works."

"I like it better when you can hear the person's voice." Especially hers, which warmed him like sunshine. "If we find out the sex of the baby beforehand, we'd only have to come up with one set of names."

"True, but—"

"Whoa." He sucked in a breath. "I get to help name this baby. There's a big responsibility. Have you started a list?"

"I thought we could work on that together while I'm here."

"But then we're back to creating two lists, since we don't know yet."

"That's right."

"We can get a start on it if you want. But seriously, why wait seven months to find out if we'll have a son or a daughter?"

"I guess I'm old-fashioned. I'd like to build the anticipation, let it be an unsolved mystery until the baby arrives. These days we can find out almost anything by hitting a key or tapping a screen. I think we need more mystery in our lives."

"Oh, we have that. It's a mystery how you got pregnant. Those condoms were brand-new, fresh out of the package."

"That's exactly what I'm talking about. We took every precaution, yet here we are. What do you make of it?"

"Poor quality control?"

"Maybe. Or maybe you and I were supposed to create a child that night."

A shiver traveled up his spine. He'd learned not to discount such things. "Like I was supposed to meet Charley."

"Do you think that's true?"

"Oh, yeah. Charley hadn't intended to go into town that day, but then Henri asked him to run a couple of errands. He spotted me parked on the square, my head under the hood of my truck."

"Engine trouble?"

"Fuel pump. I had just enough money for a new one, but I wouldn't have enough to buy food. I needed a job and Charley offered to take me on at the Buckskin. I never left."

"Maybe this baby is like that."

He gripped the wheel. "That's a nice thought, but with Charley, everything fell into place. He was looking for someone to replace an older guy who was moving to New Mexico."

"Dusty?"

"How did you know?"

"Lucy talked about him, too. She was sad to see him go since he'd been there ever since she'd started coming to the ranch with her parents."

"She told me she'd miss him. He'd been a fixture for so long. She must have been about fifteen that summer."

"Yep. It was between our freshman and sophomore year." Isabel looked over at him. "You and I almost met that summer. Lucy's parents asked me to come with them, but it didn't work out with my family's vacation plans."

He glanced at her. "I wish it had."

"I'm glad it didn't. It wouldn't have been the right time. We weren't the same people, then." She smiled. "You still had those rough edges and I didn't know who I was, yet."

"But you do, now?"

"I think so."

"I wish I could say the same. This new development has me going in circles. Maybe it was meant to be, like you said, but I don't see it falling neatly into place. I'll do my best to be a good father, but...."

"I admit there are challenges and I don't have all the answers."

"I don't have any."

"Do you think that's why you're so eager to find out if it's a boy or a girl?"

"Maybe." He took a deep breath. "Charley liked to say that learning to live with uncertainty was a valuable skill."

"And guess what? Here's a perfect chance to practice that."

"All right. You've convinced me." He slowed as the turn to the ranch appeared on his left. He waited for a pickup loaded with hay to pass in the opposite direction before crossing the road and taking the rutted dirt lane. "I don't want to know, either."

"And you're up for making two lists?"

"I guess. The naming part freaks me out. What if our kid hates what we choose?"

"I can understand feeling that way after you had to deal with Cornelius Jasper."

"What's your middle name?"

"Marie."

"Pretty."

"I like it but I wouldn't want to use it if we have a daughter. "

"Isabel?"

"Not that, either. I'd like to start from scratch."

"You don't want to consider your parents' names? Or some other relatives? Grandparents?"

"I'll think about it. Maybe. What about your mom's name?"

"Cleopatra."

"Oh, my."

"Evidently her parents were as nutty as she was about the naming thing. I never knew them or their names. They kicked her out when she became pregnant with me. Consequently, she disowned them."

"No wonder you fell in love with the Buckskin. It's solid and enduring."

"I've been thinking about that." He parked in front of the two-story ranch house so Isabel could get the key to the cabin from Henri. Another truck he didn't recognize was also parked there. "Leaving the Buckskin would be tough, but if my kid's living in Seattle, I might need to—"

"I wouldn't ask that of you." Isabel unlatched her seatbelt.

"I could find some kind of work. I'm sure they have riding stables."

"CJ, no." She swiveled in her seat to face him. "You'd never find anything near the city that's like the Buckskin. Besides, you don't like cities. You said that two months ago when the subject came up. Moving to Seattle would be too much of a sacrifice."

"I keep thinking about the Code, though."

"What code?"

"Did Lucy tell you about the Brotherhood?"

"I heard some reference to it. I assumed it was an affectionate term you guys have for each other."

"It's more than that. We formed it after Charley died, to honor him and pledge our loyalty to each other. We came up with a Code—*What Would Charley Do?* We do our best to live up to it."

Her gaze warmed. "That's wonderful. I had no idea."

"We don't go around talking about it, but now that you and I are having a baby, the Brotherhood will have your back. You can call on any of us, at any time. That will go for our child, too."

"Like the knights of old."

"Yes, ma'am. And I ask myself, would Charley leave a place he loved if it meant he could be a hands-on father to his kid?"

"But these circumstances are diff—"

"The answer is simple, Izzy. Yes, he would. I need to remember that."

6

Isabel's respect for CJ ramped up several notches. Maybe he'd been spoiled by his mother for the first sixteen years of his life, and maybe he still got cranky if he was denied something he wanted. But when the chips were down, he had the grit to seriously consider making a huge sacrifice to bond with his child.

She appreciated his willingness to do the noble thing. Unfortunately, he'd be miserable in Seattle and miserable people made poor parents. Now wasn't the time to debate it with him, though.

Reaching over, she squeezed his arm. "We'll have a week to talk about it."

He nodded. "Stay put, please." He unsnapped his seatbelt and opened his door. "I'll get you down."

His courtliness made her smile. She could get used to being treated like a queen. But she didn't dare get hooked on his cowboy ways. Or on him. She rummaged in the carryon at her feet and pulled out the pound of coffee beans she'd brought Henri.

He opened the passenger door. "Coffee?"

"For Henri. Same kind I brought when I came for the wedding. She raved about it."

"She'll appreciate that." He helped her down, his grip sure and strong.

She liked it when he touched her. She liked it way too much.

He released her hand and angled his head toward the truck parked nearby. "I think I know who that belongs to. If I'm right, you're about to meet Zane McGavin."

"Why does that name sound familiar?"

"He operates Raptors Rise in Eagles Nest."

"That's where I've heard it. Lucy told me he wants to open another raptor sanctuary up here. She can't wait."

"We're all stoked about it. Zane was scheduled to come up so he could scout out a location with Henri and Jake, who'll be managing it. I was planning to go along. Several of us were."

"Sounds like it's happening, then."

"Unless some issue crops up." He gave her a sheepish smile. "I forgot today was the day Zane would be here."

"You've had a few things on your mind."

"Yes, ma'am." He gestured toward the house. "Let's go see what happened."

When Isabel walked into the ranch house living room, Henri stood talking to a tall, good-looking cowboy. They were nearly the same height. Slim and silver-haired, Henri had an air of command that had intimidated Isabel at first.

Then Henri had revealed her sentimental side during the wedding. Her reaction to this pregnancy clinched it. Henri was a softie in disguise.

She proved it immediately by turning away from the conversation with a smile of delight. "Isabel! You're here!"

"And I brought coffee!"

"I was so hoping you would." She took the bag and gave her a hug. "I love this stuff." She turned to the tall cowboy shaking hands with CJ. "Zane, this is Isabel Ricchetti, a good friend from Seattle. Isabel, this is—"

"Zane McGavin." He tipped his hat. "At your service, Miss Isabel. I'm glad you and CJ showed up before I left."

"Me, too. It's great to meet a member of the famous McGavin clan."

He grinned. "Don't know about famous. Numerous is more like it. And increasing."

"Isabel, you have to see this." Henri left the coffee on her desk and brought over a framed five-by-seven. "Remember that little guy Hamish from the wedding?"

"How could I forget?" Isabel took the picture, which included two other children besides the baby. "Is that him? I barely recognize the little guy."

"They grow fast at this age," Zane said.

"Who are the other two?"

"My son, Rhys, and my niece, Noel. She's eighteen months and talking a blue streak. Before long she'll be telling those boys what's what."

"Cute kids. I can't believe Hamish has changed so much. He has way more hair and for sure that's a smile, not gas."

"Time goes like lightning," Zane said. "Seems like only yesterday that Rhys was born. On July second, he'll be a year old." He flashed a proud-dad smile. "He took his first steps last week."

"Hey, that's major," CJ said. "Were you there?"

"Sure was. Wouldn't have missed it. Mandy and I knew it would be any day, so we cut back on work a bit so we could coax him along. He didn't need much encouragement. He was ready."

"Cool." CJ moved closer to Isabel and studied the five-by-seven. "Rhys is six months younger than Noel, but he's bigger." He smiled at Zane. "Chip off the old block, huh?"

"Guess so."

CJ focused on the picture again. "Can't believe the change in Hamish. Must be something, watching them grow."

"Very exciting. Worth every sleepless night and postponed project. We'd like to give Rhys a sister or brother. We'll see how that goes."

"I have a younger sister." Isabel handed the picture back to Henri. "We're close in age, which is nice. I can't imagine what life would be like without her." Would her baby have any siblings? Not full-blooded ones, for sure, and a big age gap was likely, too.

"My wife Mandy is an only," Zane said. "Although she had me and my brothers next door, she still would have liked a sister or brother."

"I'm an only, too," CJ said. "I used to wish for the same thing." He shrugged and slid a glance at Isabel. "Not always in the cards." He held her gaze for a beat before turning back to Zane. "So what happened today? Did you guys find a good location for the visitor center?"

"We sure did." Zane's phone chimed. "Excuse me a minute." He glanced at the screen. "I'll let Henri tell you about it. If I don't get a move on, I'll screw up date night." He tucked his phone away. "Nice meeting you, Isabel. Henri, we have more to iron out, but I love the plan so far. You will, too, CJ." He tipped his hat to the women and clapped CJ on the shoulder before hurrying out the door.

CJ faced Henri, his expression eager. "So? Are we ready to break ground?"

"We are." Henri's eyes glowed with excitement. "Isabel, I don't know if Lucy—"

"She did. She's thrilled about it."

"For good reason. It's an awesome concept. And now we know where it'll be. As the one who'll manage the day-to-day operation, Jake got final say, but he agreed it was perfect."

"If it's the clearing I'm thinking of," CJ said, "it's close to the cabin he and Millie are building."

"That's the one."

"I'm not surprised they got together." Isabel smiled. "Sparks were flying during the wedding weekend."

Henri laughed. "That pretty much describes their relationship in all its facets. They're watching how-to videos as they work together on the cabin. It's been...interesting." She exchanged a glance with CJ. "I still can't believe they've moved in already. They might as well be camping out."

"Matt and Lucy are in the same boat with theirs. They're still cooking on a camp stove."

"I know." Henri sighed. "Impatient kids. I told both couples they could stay in a guest cabin until their places were more livable, but..." She shrugged and glanced at Isabel. "Enough chit-chat. I'll bet you're ready to put your feet up."

"I admit I'm a little tired."

"Then let me fetch your key." She walked over to the antique desk that was clearly action central for the Buckskin. Positioning the framed picture in a place of honor, she plucked a key out of a drawer and brought it over. "Millie set up your cabin today, but if you need anything she didn't think of, please let us know."

"I can't imagine what that would be. And thank you for your generosity. Despite what you said in your email, I feel that I should pay for—"

"Let me do this, Isabel. You can repay me by bringing the baby for a visit now and then. And sending lots of pictures in between times."

"Of course I will."

"Then we'll be even. CJ will see that you get settled, but we're all here for you."

Her throat tightened. "Thank you. I didn't realize how close-knit everyone was."

"CJ told you about the Brotherhood?"

"He did."

"You can count on those men, Isabel. And on me."

She nodded and swallowed the lump in her throat. Her emotions weren't under the best of control these days. Much more of this talk and she'd dissolve into a weepy mess. She turned to CJ. "It's been a long day. We'd better go."

"Right. Let's do it." He glanced at Henri. "I'm happy about that raptor center."

"Me, too. We'll talk more about it tomorrow."

"Yes, ma'am." He put on his hat and touched two fingers to the brim before escorting Isabel out the door and handing her into his truck.

After he closed the door and rounded the truck to climb behind the wheel, he turned toward her. "Are you okay?"

"I'm fine. Just a little weary. Didn't sleep much last night."

"Me, either." He buckled up and started the engine. "Dinner will be served in the dining hall in an hour or so, but if you're not up to going, I could bring you something from the buffet."

"That's a lovely idea, but I don't trust either of us in that situation."

"Okay, then I'll leave it by your door."

"You don't need to—"

"Yes, ma'am, I do. I feel a strong urge to do something for you. Two months ago, that would have involved giving you multiple orgasms, but since that's not an option, I'll at least bring you dinner."

7

After reluctantly leaving Isabel at her cabin, CJ texted Kate, the dining hall cook, to alert her he'd be picking up a dinner from the buffet for Isabel. He'd need a couple of to-go boxes.

She texted right back. *Just one dinner?*

Just one. I'll be eating in the bunkhouse. And sleeping there, too.

Is there a problem?

He looked at the question and laughed. *Don't get me started.*

Kate sent back a sad face emoji.

Yeah, that just about summed it up. He and Izzy had been on the same page two months ago and now they weren't even reading the same book.

Normally he'd be on duty helping Garrett, the new hire, with making dinner for the wranglers, but he'd asked to be excused. He'd expected to be sharing a meal with Izzy.

He could show up and announce that he was available to help fix dinner, after all, but if he went to the barn instead, Rafe and Jake would be there feeding the horses. He could speak freely with them. Garrett was an okay guy, but he'd only been on board two months. He wasn't a part of the Brotherhood, at least not yet.

CJ parked beside the old hip-roofed barn. He'd loved it on sight when Charley had brought him here ten years ago. Might be his favorite structure on the ranch property.

After helping replace the fuel pump, Charley had led him out to the ranch and introduced him to Henri. She hadn't blinked an eye when Charley had announced they had a new wrangler. They'd had complete trust in each other's decisions.

Maybe that had always been true and maybe the trust had developed over time. CJ had never asked. Until now, the dynamics of a good marriage hadn't mattered to him.

After the meeting with Henri, Charley had brought him to the barn and tested him on his knowledge. Then he'd explained his belief in treating horses as equal partners. It was the first of many lessons, some hard, some easy.

Missing Charley was less painful after four years without the guy. CJ would give anything for a heart-to-heart now, but at least he had the Brotherhood. Climbing down from the truck, he walked through the open double doors.

Jake came toward him pushing a wheelbarrow loaded with hay flakes. He paused. "What're you doing here?"

"Slight change of plans. Let me get some gloves and I'll help you." He ducked into the tack room and grabbed a pair.

"Did I see CJ come through the door?" Rafe called from the back of the barn.

"It's either CJ or his doppelganger!" Jake hollered back.

"Hey, CJ, did you have a fight with Isabel?"

"No fight!" He put on the gloves as he walked out of the tack room.

Rafe abandoned his wheelbarrow and headed down the aisle. At six-six, he could walk it quicker than any of them. "I need the story on this deal, bro."

"Izzy wants us to co-parent this baby as friends, not lovers. That way we can each find someone else more suited to us."

Rafe frowned. "Did she? Is that what—"

"Not yet, but she thinks that's the way this should go. Getting frisky during this trip would be contrary to the plan so she's called a halt to those activities."

"Well, damn." Jake heaved a sigh. "Are you on board with this idea?"

"Doesn't matter. She gets to make the call. But for the record, no, I'm not. The more I think about this baby, the more I want to be involved in my kid's life."

"And hers?" Rafe met his gaze.

"Yes, which means I may have to relocate."

"To *Seattle*?" Jake's horrified expression brought a snort of laughter from Rafe.

"You say that like he's heading off to the dark side of the moon."

"Might as well be. It's a big city. Coastal. From what I hear, all the guest ranches are in Eastern Washington."

Rafe nudged back his hat. "I think that's true. When we went down to Eagles Nest for Seth and Zoe's wedding in January, I talked with Kendra McGavin's husband. I think he's from Spokane. That's where you find ranches."

"So I'll hire on at a riding stable. I'll bet they have some of those."

"I'll guess a lot of 'em ride English." Rafe peered at him. "You okay with that?"

"Riding is riding."

"Not in my opinion," Jake said. "Those tiny saddles don't feel right. My boys don't care for them at all. No good resting spot. No wonder the hunter-jumper dudes are posting all the damn time. But that's not the worst of it. Didn't Isabel say she lives in an apartment near her coffee shop?"

"She does. She can walk to the shop."

"In downtown Seattle." Jake eyed him. "You won't sleep a wink with all that traffic."

Rafe laughed. "I don't think sleep is what he's after, Jake, old man. Are you telling me the thrill has worn off now that you're with Millie every night?"

"*No.* But after we have fun, the only thing we hear outside the cabin is an owl hooting or a coyote yipping. That's all I care to hear. I'd go nuts with cars honking and sirens wailing and brakes screeching."

"I'll wear earplugs."

"Hmm." Jake studied him. "You seem to be semi-convinced this is the route to take, and yet you're here and not with Isabel. Could it be she's not excited about your proposed move to Seattle?"

"She says I'll be miserable."

"Smart lady."

"I'll be miserable either way, so I might as well be with her and my kid."

Jake rolled his eyes. "I'm sure she can't wait to get your grumpy self in residence. What a treat to have an unhappy guy hanging around all the time."

"I wouldn't be grumpy, damn it."

"Oh, well, then." Rafe glanced at Jake and grinned. "Nothing to worry about."

"Hey. I'm better than I used to be."

"I'll give you that," Jake said. "You were a spoiled brat when you first arrived. Now you hardly ever get that look on your face."

"Yeah." Rafe chuckled. "Like someone just snatched your all-day sucker."

"I'll have you know that Lucy told Isabel I was sweet."

"You are, and you were even back then, *if* you got your way. Lucy doesn't know you like we do."

He sighed. "I get the idea you think going to Seattle would be a mistake."

"Huge mistake." Jake's expression softened. "Look, your heart's in the right place, but you don't even enjoy going into Great Falls. You won't be much of an asset to Isabel or your kid if your jaw is clenched twenty-four-seven. And I think it would be."

"You could be right. Listen, we're making the horses wait for their dinner. Charley would tell us to feed first, jawbone later."

Rafe nodded. "He would. Let's get 'er done."

An hour later, CJ picked up the to-go box from Kate in the dining hall kitchen. She'd taken to wearing a chef's hat over her short blond curls. Cute.

She gave him a quick smile. "I'm sure you'll get it worked out."

"Have you talked to Rafe already?"

"No. I just assumed there's an issue to be handled. Does Rafe know what it is?"

"Yes. Tell him I said he's free to explain. I don't care who knows. Maybe the Buckskin hive mind will come up with a solution." He lifted the paper bag. "Thanks for this." He tipped his hat. "I'm off."

8

"I'm not surprised CJ's ready to move to Seattle." Lucy settled into one of the Adirondack chairs on the guest cabin's front porch and put a leather satchel containing her pencils and sketchpad next to her. A pound of her favorite coffee sat on the table between the chairs. "He's very tender-hearted."

Isabel took the other chair. "You know him better than I do. The way he talked about Apple Grove and the Buckskin back in April, I thought nothing could make him leave. I was sure he'd see the logic of my plan."

"This isn't about logic, Iz."

"Not anymore." She exhaled and leaned against the slanted back of the chair. "Thanks for coming over."

"Of course. I didn't earlier because I thought you two would be getting cozy in the cabin." She ran her fingers through her frosted hair. "Matt thought so, too, judging from CJ's excitement about seeing you again."

"Clearly he was counting on that. And here's the sad part. His reaction to the pregnancy and his relationship with me is what every woman longs for. He's all in, doesn't want to miss a thing, wants to move on to some kind of commitment." She turned her head to meet Lucy's gaze. "You should have seen his face when he held Amy this afternoon. I melted."

"He'll make a great dad."

"I *know.* That's the hell of it. He won't be happy with the kind of part-time gig the situation calls for. But I can't encourage this Seattle plan. It would be a disaster."

Lucy nodded. "Yep."

"It's a damned mess, Luce. I've always prided myself on making good choices, but—"

"Are you wishing you hadn't spent the night with him?"

"No. We had a wonderful time and I'm not sorry about the baby. I had it all worked out. For the first few years, CJ and I would visit back and forth. When the kid's older, he or she could spend more time at the ranch, maybe whole summers."

"Nice picture."

"It could be, but not if the man is Cornelius Jasper Andrews."

"Excuse me?"

"Whoops. I should have asked him if—"

Lucy grinned. "Cornelius Jasper?"

"Yes, but it might be a secret."

"I wonder if Matt knows."

"You'd think he would, right?"

"If he does, he never mentioned it to me."

"I'll ask CJ if it's common knowledge in the Brotherhood. For now, don't say anything to Matt."

"I won't. But guys are funny, aren't they? As Millie said during one of our girls' night gab sessions, they divulge info on a need-to-know basis."

"Which explains why he told me. I needed to know for the birth certificate."

"Did he say where the name comes from?"

"Yes, but I'd better not—oh, look. Speak of the devil. Why is he—oh, right. Dinner."

"You're having dinner with him?"

"No, but he insisted on bringing me a meal from the dining hall. I spaced it. My mom warned me I might have pregnancy brain when the hormones kick in."

"I've heard of that. But if your brain isn't working right, the rest of you looks great. You're glowing. My guess is that CJ's Seattle plan is partly that he wants to be with you."

"And I'd be fine with that, but he's a cowboy through-and-through." As his truck pulled in, eagerness to see him made her twitchy. "Asking him to live in a Seattle apartment would be like coaxing a creature of the forest into a cage."

"Well, you have six days to hammer out some kind of compromise." Lucy stood, picked up her leather satchel and the bag of coffee. "Thanks for this. You know how I love it."

"You're welcome." She left her chair, too. "Are you leaving?"

"You know what they say. Three's a crowd."

"Hey, you don't have to go." With Lucy here, this inconvenient reaction to CJ could be papered over. "He's just dropping off food. We—"

"Six days isn't all that long, considering the magnitude of the problem. You two need time to evaluate all the possibilities."

"No, we don't. There aren't that many possibilities and only one that makes sense." If the agile way he swung down from the cab of his truck made her heart stutter, she did *not* need to be alone with the guy.

Lucy's knowing smile was easy to interpret. "You do realize you're nuts about him."

"That's irrelevant, Luce. We aren't right for each other."

"Matt believed the same thing about us. Time and circumstances proved him wrong."

"Hang around for a few minutes. At least until he's gone."

"Isabel Marie Ricchetti! I never took you for a coward."

"I blame the hormones." She glanced in CJ's direction. "Don't leave me alone with him."

"Iz, if you're determined not to have sex with the guy, you'll have to tough that out on your own. I'm not going to be your chaperone." She turned to face CJ. "Hi, there, cowboy! Izzy says you're on a mission of mercy, since she's eating for two, now."

"That's why I asked Kate for a double portion, since Izzy's incubating the next generation."

"Let me remind you the incubator is right here." Isabel crossed her arms over her chest. "And she'd like a more flattering description of her condition, please."

Lucy grinned. "What would you prefer? Me, I've always liked *broody*. But *enceinte* is classier, so if you'd rather—"

"Your time will come, Luce, and I'll be ready."

"Ah, Izzy, I tease because I have a touch of envy. Matt and I aren't ready to have a baby yet, but I look forward to the day."

"Hey, I can save baby stuff for you."

"That would be awesome." She gave Isabel a hug. "Want to do something tomorrow while CJ is tied up with ranch chores? I sketch in the morning, but I can block out a couple of hours in the afternoon."

"That would work for me. I've scheduled a video chat with Naomi in the morning to check on things at the shop. Do you think I could get an afternoon hair appointment at Tres Beau? I love your cut. I'd like something similar."

"I could use a trim, myself. That would be fun. I'll check in the morning and see what Josette and Eva have available." She started down the porch steps. "See you guys later."

"Need a lift back to your cabin?" CJ paused on his way to the porch. "I'm just the dinner delivery guy. I'm not staying."

"Thanks for the offer, but I love trekking around the ranch." She held up her satchel. "That's why I brought this, in case I get inspired on my way home."

He smiled. "Okay, then. Henri told me about the raptor center. Great news."

"Isn't it? Can't wait. See you guys!" Lifting the bag of coffee, she called out another *thank you* and set off for her half-finished cabin.

And she was lucky enough to share that cabin with the love of her life. Now Isabel was the one dealing with envy. She turned to face CJ. "I forgot you were coming."

"You did? But that was only—"

"A little more than an hour ago. I know. I've been told the hormone dump that happens during pregnancy alters a woman's brain chemistry and I might not always think clearly."

He gazed at her. "That must be tough for you. You're always so ahead of the game."

"Tell me about it. I'm navigating this very tricky situation and I might not have all my marbles, at least not until it's too late and I've made some really dumb decisions."

"If I can help in any way, just say the word."

"I don't expect you to be my keeper. That's an unfair burden. But if you see me heading for a cliff, feel free to intervene."

"Will do." He handed her the bag of food. "So you want to get your hair cut as short as Lucy's?"

"At least that short. Summer's coming and I'll be carrying baby weight. I don't need to be taking the extra time and effort to wash and dry all this." She lifted a strand of her hair away from her shoulder.

He nodded. "I get that."

"But you're not happy about the idea."

"Your hair is beautiful. Shiny and soft. That's one of the things I remember from that night, how it felt on my..." He swallowed. "Guess that's not an appropriate thing to say."

"Guess not." One subtle reference to their lovemaking and she was on fire. Backing away was the wise thing to do. Her feet weren't cooperating. They moved her a step closer.

His gray eyes turned thundercloud dark. Lifting his hand, he cupped her cheek. "I have the feeling you don't want me to go."

"I don't." Taking a shaky breath, she moved out of reach. "But it's for the best."

He shoved both hands in the pockets of his jeans. His chest heaved as his hot gaze met hers. "This isn't going to work, Izzy. It's obvious you want me as much as I want you. I can't see us accomplishing much when we're both craving something you claim we can't have."

"I underestimated the strength of our chemistry."

"No kidding."

"And my overactive hormones aren't helping. I didn't consider that, either."

"Well, now you know. I must be picking up on your hormonal overload because the minute I come within ten feet, I want to kiss the living daylights out of you. And damned if you don't look like that would suit you just fine."

"Let me think about this."

"What good is that going to do? It won't change anything. I say let's end this torture. Let me take you to bed."

"No. I promised myself that—"

"Okay." He backed away. "I'm leaving, but this isn't over. We have a bunch of hurdles, but we can't deal with them until we deal with this." Turning, he walked back around his truck, climbed in and shut the door with a little more force than was necessary.

She was shaking so badly she had to clutch the bag in both hands to keep from dropping it. Heart pounding, she hurried inside as he gunned the truck and pulled out. He was right, damn it. But his solution wasn't a solution at all. It would only make things worse.

9

CJ slept with his phone under his pillow, but Izzy didn't call. First thing in the morning he texted her. *Thought I'd round up the gang for a night at the Choosy Moose. Want to go with us?*

He used *us* instead of *me* on purpose. Didn't want it to look like a date or a subtle way to wear her down. Even if it was both. In April, their attraction had blossomed on the dance floor at the Moose. Evidently he'd have to engage in some courting behavior if he wanted to turn this situation around.

Charley had taught him to listen carefully to what people said about themselves. Izzy had told him she was old-fashioned, which was why she didn't want to know the sex of their baby.

But the arrangement she'd suggested, long-distance parenting on his part, was a modern wrinkle. What if she secretly longed for him to be a true partner in the process, a full-time dad and a devoted husband? If so, he could tap into that.

Maybe he was old-fashioned, too. He and Izzy had accidentally created a family and he wanted to keep that family together. And why not? He lusted after the mother of his child. Evidently she had similar feelings for him. They'd created fertile ground for developing deeper feelings, good for them and good for the baby.

But she'd convinced herself that living six-hundred miles apart was the way to go. He had to change her mind. First step, get her back in his arms while a country song helped create some down-home magic.

She was susceptible to that. So was he. If they could fall in love a little bit during her stay, she might begin to question the wisdom of living separate lives.

His phone pinged with her reply. *That sounds nice. What time?*

It'll be after dinner. I'll check with everyone and let you know. See you then.

She sent him a thumbs-up emoji. Not the most romantic of gestures, but he'd take it. Now to rally the troops.

He'd start with Matt, who shared morning barn duty with him. Matt was a good place to begin, since he'd logged in more years at the ranch than any member of the Brotherhood except Seth, who'd moved to Eagles Nest. Matt had taken over Seth's leadership position.

But the subject was too important to broach during the feeding routine. He wanted Matt's full attention. He'd make use of the lull between feeding and turnout.

After leaning his wheelbarrow against the back wall of the barn, he waited for Matt to do the same. "Need to discuss something with you, bro."

Matt pulled off his work gloves. "Bet I can guess what's on your mind. Lucy gave me some details last night."

"Good. Saves time." He tucked his gloves in his back pocket. "Bottom line, I need to change Izzy's mind about this plan of hers."

"Are you serious about a move to Seattle?"

"I'll do whatever it takes to keep our little family together."

Matt glanced at him. "Have you told Isabel that?"

"Not yet. But I don't see any other way to make sure I'm a big part of that kid's life."

"And Isabel's?"

"That, too. I think we could make it as a couple."

"Under different circumstances, I agree you two would have a shot. But like everybody else has said, I can't see you adapting well to city life."

"I will if the alternative is watching Izzy marry some dude in Seattle who'll spend more time with my kid than I will."

Matt sighed. "Yeah, that would suck."

"She'll want to have another kid with him, too."

"How do you know?"

"Zane was up at the house talking to Henri yesterday when Izzy and I arrived. He mentioned that he and Mandy were trying for kid number two and Izzy agreed that having a sibling is the way to go."

"Lucy said that Isabel envisions you marrying someone local and having the family you want in the rural atmosphere you love. It's a generous attitude on her part. And I see her point."

"Oh, I see it, too. That was the plan when she left. But the baby changed my thinking. Then I saw her walking toward me in the terminal yesterday. I want her as much as I ever did. More."

Matt nodded. "Lucy thinks Isabel's still hung up on you. And she wants you to be happy."

"I want that for her, too. I'm arrogant enough to believe she'll be happy with me."

"Okay, then."

"I just have to convince her we belong together."

"How are you planning to go about it?"

"That's what I wanted to talk to you about."

"Sounds like you're considering a Brotherhood campaign."

"I am."

Matt paused and adjusted the fit of his hat. "If we succeed in changing Isabel's mind, we'll lose you."

"Not completely. I won't live here anymore, but I'll come back for visits as often as I can."

"Yeah, well…" Sadness filled his gaze. "The thing is I'm kinda used to your ugly mug, Cornelius."

He smiled. "Start using that name and I'll be obliged to rearrange yours."

"You tried that once. And I won, as I recall."

"But you're a married man, now. Everybody knows married men get soft. I could take you, no problem."

Matt laughed. "In your dreams, cowboy." He sighed again and scuffed his boot against a piece of straw stuck to the barn's wooden floor. Then he glanced up. "This is what you really want?"

"Yes, sir."

"Let's move these ponies out to the pasture. We can continue this discussion while we're mucking out stalls. I think better when I'm shoveling."

"Me, too."

* * *

"Why can't Isabel just move here?" Nick climbed into the cramped backseat of CJ's truck.

"Because of her coffee shop." CJ waited for Garrett to swing up into the passenger seat before starting the engine.

"Couldn't she sell it?"

"That would be like cutting off her right arm, bro. She made a go of that business despite fierce competition from the big dogs."

"Big dogs is right." Garrett laid his hat on his lap. "Seattle's home to some famous coffee companies. I'm impressed she carved out a place for herself."

"So am I," Nick said. "She's thriving in that city. I just can't picture you thriving there, CJ.

While I was lifting weights today I watched a video of the place on my phone. It looked nice, just not right for you. It's all seafood, ferries and jazz festivals. I didn't see anybody wearing a Stetson. Lots of umbrellas, though."

"It's right for me if Izzy and my kid are there."

"Makes sense." Garrett glanced at him. "I'd do the same in your shoes. And I'd work hard to adapt."

"You might be able to at this point, Garrett," Nick said, "but wait until you've lived here for as many years as CJ and I have. The Buckskin gets in your blood. I'm afraid he'll move there, marry Isabel and realize too late that he's in the wrong place."

"I'll take that chance."

Nick let out a breath. "Then you have my support, bro. Like Matt said, we'll do our part to facilitate this romance."

"Speaking of that, are all the Babes coming to the Moose?"

"Oh, you know it. The only thing they love better than their own schemes is watching one of ours play out. They also want to apprise Isabel of their great-auntie status. I've heard rumors of a baby shower this week."

"That's nice." CJ slowed the truck as they approached the town square. Usually on a Tuesday night the grassy area around the gazebo was empty and quiet. Instead the clatter of several folks putting together various sizes of wooden structures filled the air. "What's going on?"

"Your head must be in the clouds," Nick said. "This weekend is the Founders Day celebration."

"I totally forgot that was coming up. How many years is it?"

"I dunno."

"I'll look it up." Garrett pulled out his phone and tapped on it a few times. "A hundred and fifty-two. What happens on Founders Day weekend?"

"All kinds of stuff." CJ put on his turn signal and waited for a truck to back out of a spot right in front of the Moose. Good sign that he'd scored it. If all went well, he'd be ushering Izzy out the front door and into his truck in about two hours. He shut off the engine.

"Just think, bro." Nick unlatched his seatbelt and leaned forward. "Could be your last Founders Day celebration."

"Nick, stop it." He opened his door.

"I just want you to consider everything before you make such a life-changing decision."

"I've already made it. I just need Isabel to come on board." He and Garrett exited the truck and waited on the sidewalk for Nick to climb out of the backseat. "Nice night."

Garrett nodded. "Feels good to ditch our jackets for a change."

Nick stepped up on the curb and settled his hat on his head. "Don't look now, but Matt just grabbed a space in front of Gertie's. Your lady-love has arrived."

"I noticed." The transportation plan for tonight had been choreographed over dinner. Matt had invited Izzy to ride with him, Lucy, Jake and Millie. Rafe was bringing Kate and Leo, leaving room for Nick and Garrett in his truck if CJ took Izzy home early.

"There's Rafe," Garrett said. "Looks like he'll have to park in back. Do you want to wait for Matt and company or go in?

CJ took a steadying breath and tugged his hat a bit lower. "Let's wait."

"You said you didn't want to look too eager to see her."

"But I don't want to act like I'm avoiding her, either. I'll keep it cool. I want to see what she did with her hair today. She was getting it cut."

"I hope not too short," Nick said. "It's gorgeous long."

"I know."

Jake helped Millie out of the back and then assisted Izzy. She stepped down and laughed at something Jake said. She wore a bright yellow shirt with a hem that reached to her hips, snug jeans and boots. Clearly Lucy had taken her shopping after the salon appointment.

Her hair was shorter, chin-length instead of reaching her shoulders. For a second, he grieved the loss of the silken strands that had caressed his body when they'd made love.

Then she tossed her head and the sassy swing of her dark hair sent a message straight to his groin. He gulped.

"You're staring, bro," Nick murmured.

"I didn't expect the haircut would make her even sexier than before."

"You want to ditch the program and just go for it?"

"No. She'd only dig in her heels if I come on too strong. Stick with the plan. I'll... manage."

"Count your breaths," Garrett said.

"Count my breaths?"

"Try it. Works for me."

"Okay." *One. Two. Three. Four. Five. Six.* Sure enough, he was back in control. "Thanks, Garrett. Good tip."

"Works while you're having sex, too, whenever you're worried about your timing."

Nick glanced at him. "Really?"

"In my case, anyway."

"I believe you. I don't have a girlfriend so I can't test it. CJ might be able to, though. Hey, bro, if it works for you, let me know, okay?"

"No can do."

"Why not?"

He flashed Nick a grin. "I always have perfect timing." Especially with Izzy. Although if she kept ramping up her hotness factor, she might make a liar out of him. And he wouldn't mind a bit. But first the Brotherhood campaign had to succeed.

10

He's up to something. An hour into the evening and CJ still hadn't asked for a dance. Not that Isabel had been left without partners. She'd been on the floor for nearly every number.

The Buckskin Brotherhood knew their dance moves and seemed eager to demonstrate their specialties. Leo, the classically handsome wrangler, loved to waltz. The two-step was Rafe's favorite, and he was surprisingly agile for such a big man. Afterward he apologized if he'd worn her out. He had, but she wouldn't admit it.

Matt had a classic country style that relaxed her, and Jake kept her laughing through the entire number. Garrett was a terrific dancer. She'd seen him clear the floor with other partners. But he toned it way down with her, evidently worried that he'd overtax her.

Nick didn't have that concern. He had his own athletic version of country swing—fun but challenging. He was also the one who insisted she sit out for a while, though.

He escorted her back to the large booth the Brotherhood had commandeered and ordered her popcorn and a bottle of non-alcoholic cider.

When she made quick work of the popcorn, he ordered fries and nachos.

"Popcorn was plenty, Nick. You didn't have to order something else."

"Oh, yes, I did. It's for me as much as you. Dancing works up an appetite, although in my case, that's easy to do. I'm always hungry."

She grinned. "Then you must be pregnant."

"If I am, I'll never have to work another day in my life. A few rounds of the talk-show circuit, a bestselling memoir, and I'll retire to devote my time to the miracle baby."

"You'd retire and give up ranch work?"

"Nah, you're right. I'd hang onto that. Nothing like the scent of fresh horse poop in the morning. Starts the day off right, y'know?"

"You can't fool me. You love your job."

He nodded. "Very much."

"I assume you've heard about CJ's crazy idea of moving to Seattle."

"Yes, ma'am."

"It's ridiculous, right?"

"Doesn't matter if I think so. It's CJ's life. He knows what he needs better'n me."

"Then again, maybe he's given up on the idea."

"Oh?"

"He asked me to join you guys for an evening at the Moose, so I assumed he'd pick me up. Instead, Matt turned out to be my ride. Then we get here, and CJ hasn't said more than five words to me since we walked through the door."

"He hasn't been rude, has he?"

"Not at all. Very polite. Nice smile. I just expected... more contact with him, I suppose."

"Well, I do have some inside info on that."

"Can I pry it out of you?"

"No prying necessary. He told me he's giving you some space. He said I was free to tell you that if you asked."

"Space for what?"

"Whatever folks need space for. I never understood that concept."

That made her laugh. "Technically I need space because I'm expanding by the minute, but I doubt that's what CJ—"

"Seriously?" His gaze dropped briefly to her stomach. Then he looked up, clearly fascinated by the concept. "By the minute?"

"By the second, in fact, or the millisecond. The baby is growing at a steady pace."

"Makes sense, but I never thought of it that way. While we're sitting here waiting for fries and nachos, your baby is growing."

"It's mind-blowing, right?"

"Yes, ma'am. I thought only two of us were in this booth, but turns out there's one more."

"And because of that third person, I'll pick the chili peppers off because they might be too much for the little tyke."

"I should have thought of that and told them no peppers. I'll take them off for you. I love 'em."

"I've heard about your legendary fondness for all things edible. Is there anything you *don't* like?"

"Anchovies."

"But they're delicious!"

"I suppose you eat them in Seattle."

"I do."

"Because you're all about seafood and such?"

"Absolutely. I love all kinds."

"I wonder if CJ's thought about that."

"He doesn't like it?"

"I'm sure canned tuna's fine with him, and we've had baked salmon a few times since Garrett started handling the cooking. Jake never fixed it." He shrugged. "For all I know, he'll discover he likes seafood. I just wonder if he's considered that angle."

"What angle?" CJ slipped into the horseshoe-shaped booth, but on the opposite end, putting him about as far from her as he could get and still be at the same table.

"Folks eat a lot of anchovies in Seattle," Nick said. "Isabel loves them."

"I didn't know that." His gray eyes twinkled as he glanced at her. "Plain or with other stuff?"

"Either." She held his gaze. He looked extremely handsome tonight. The pearl-gray shirt might be new. She'd never seen him wearing it. "I can eat them right out of the jar."

He didn't flinch. "I'll have to try that sometime."

"You won't like them, especially plain," Nick said. "You couldn't handle those sardines Leo brought from Great Falls that time. Anchovies are even—"

"That was at least five years ago." He continued to focus on her, his expression calm, his smile friendly. "I've matured. My palate has matured. Anyway, I just came by to see if you need anything, Iz."

"I'm good, thanks. Nick's ordered a basket of fries and a plate of nachos."

"Yeah, bro," Nick gestured toward the server coming their way. "Feel free to stick around and have some. Get yourself a cider. I thought Isabel needed a break."

He nodded. "Good idea. Enjoy." He stood. "Appreciate the invite, but I just remembered I promised Henri I'd dance this number with her. I'll check back later." Touching two fingers to the brim of his hat, he made eye contact one last time before walking away.

She didn't want him to go. She wanted him to promise a dance to her, too. Her neediness was damned embarrassing.

His loose-hipped stride took him over to the table occupied by Henri and her five best friends. He offered his hand to Henri, led her to the dance floor and whirled her into a lively two step. They danced well together.

Her throat tightened. After the way they'd parted the night before, she couldn't fault him for distancing himself. But she didn't have to like it.

"You really care about him."

She turned back to Nick. His knowing expression left her no room to maneuver. "I really do. Which is why I'm against this move to Seattle."

"To be honest, I didn't think he'd take to being a father this quick or be so determined to be fully involved."

"I didn't either. But when you get right down to it, I don't know him all that well."

"I thought I did. Then again, I've never seen him faced with something like this before." He gestured to the nachos. "While you were watching him, I took off all the peppers and ate 'em."

She glanced at the plate and laughed. "You and I are a pair, Nick. Odds are we can hoover up food better than anybody in this joint."

He grinned back at her. "I'm glad to finally meet someone who's as food-driven as I am."

"You need to hang out with more pregnant ladies." She started in on the nachos.

She and Nick had finished those and the basket of fries when Leo came to claim another waltz. And the rotation continued as before.

When Jake invited her out on the floor, the song was an easy two-step that allowed for conversation. "Did you guys plan this dancing-with-Isabel thing in advance?"

"Yes."

"Jake! Now I feel like a charity case."

"The exact opposite. You're a favorite. We had to divvy you up fairly so we wouldn't squabble in front of you."

"Come on, Jake."

"It's true. You're fun to dance with. None of us wanted to waste this golden opportunity."

"Except CJ."

"CJ has issues."

"Don't we all. I was hoping he and I could be friends, but that's turning out to be more difficult than I thought."

"So he's said."

"You'd think we could dance together at least once tonight. I'm not sure how much longer we'll be here since everybody has to get up for work. I wonder if he was planning to ask at all."

"You could ask him, instead."

"Yes, I could. I don't know why I didn't think of that. I'll blame pregnancy brain." *Or pride.* "If he turns me down, then—"

"He won't. That's not CJ."

"You're right. Thanks for the suggestion." She surveyed the couples on the floor. "He's dancing with the woman who owns the indoor riding arena."

"That's Ed."

"I need to catch him before he takes her back to the table where the Babes are. If I don't, he's liable to ask one of the others. That's mostly who he's danced with."

"Yes, ma'am. I'll make sure we're within range of CJ and Ed when the song ends."

"You're a pal, Jake."

"We'll have to double-time it to get there, though. Hold on." Dodging and weaving through the dancers, he twirled her for a dramatic finish that left her face-to-face with CJ as the last notes of the song trailed off.

He exchanged a look with Jake. No telling what unspoken message it conveyed, but it obviously meant something.

Breathing fast from the accelerated pace, she touched CJ's arm and gasped out her question. "May I have the next dance?"

His gray gaze lit up. "I'd be honored."

_11_

For the past half-hour, CJ had been itching to dance with Izzy. But the Brotherhood had advised him to hold off. Matt had finally given him the go-ahead and he'd planned to approach her after escorting Ed back to the table. She'd beat him to it. Bonus.

There was the matter of returning Ed, though.

"I've got this," Jake murmured. Turning, he bowed to Ed. "May I have this dance, ma'am?"

Ed grinned. "Certainly, son. CJ got me all warmed up. Think you can handle a hot Babe like me?"

"I doubt it, but I'm more than willing to try."

Shaking with anticipation, CJ turned to Izzy. He'd given the band specific instructions and added a generous tip. Right on cue, they played the opening chords of his requested song, Tim McGraw's _She's My Kind of Rain._ He held Izzy's gaze and slowly drew her into his arms.

As the lyrics spilled over them, he began to move. He longed to tuck her in tight, but that part was up to her. The glow in her dark eyes brightened, filling him with so much joy he could barely breathe.

Gradually she eliminated the distance between them. When her body finally nestled against his and she locked her hands behind his neck, he settled his clasped hands at the small of her back. So sweet. So perfect.

"I gave up on you asking me."

"I was about to."

"That's what they all say."

"I wanted to give you—"

"Space?" The corners of her plump, kissable mouth turned up.

He nodded.

"But you invited me to go along tonight."

"You'd said you wanted an evening at the Choosy Moose."

"Mostly to dance with you. It's one of the things we do best."

"The second-best thing."

She rolled her eyes.

"Well, it is."

"Yeah, okay." She favored him with a tiny smile.

"Your hair looks great."

"Thanks. Eva did a good job. She said to tell you hello." Her body brushed his in a gentle, sensual rhythm.

"I like how she cuts my hair."

"I think she has a slight crush."

"I don't encourage her."

"Why not?"

"My interests lie elsewhere." Time to switch topics. "How's Naomi doing at the shop?"

"Just fine."

So much for that conversational thread. "I noticed you picked up boots today. Like 'em?"

"Yep. Comfier than my high-heeled ones. Bought a hat, too."

"Sounds like you're ready to ride."

"Tomorrow. With Lucy and Matt."

"So I heard."

"You did?"

"Word gets around."

"Hm." Her gaze turned speculative. "This song... I'm trying to remember if I mentioned it to you back in April."

"You might have." He'd learned it, could have asked the band to let him sit in and play it with them. Choosing between showboating on stage or holding Izzy on the dance floor had been easy.

"Is it a coincidence they're playing it now?"

"No, ma'am. I promised myself I'd have at least one dance with you. When I knew for sure the time was coming up, I requested it."

"So you really were about to ask me?"

"I was."

"That's very romantic."

"I'm a romantic guy."

"I'm beginning to see that. You remembered we danced to it at the wedding reception."

"And you said it reminds you of the misty rain in Seattle, which is fun to walk in without an umbrella, especially when it's warm."

"I said all that?"

"Uh-huh."

"I guess the champagne loosened my tongue."

"You were fun that night. A little crazy, but—"

"Maybe too crazy."

"Not really. You mellowed out toward the end of the evening. Then the band played this. It was a turning point. For me, anyway."

Her voice softened. "And me. Dancing with you to this song was... a special moment."

"All the moments were special." He took a slow breath and let it out. "Izzy... can I take you home?"

She stiffened. "Is that what—"

"It's not what you think. I won't come in."

"You won't?"

Was there a trace of disappointment in her voice? "I thought we'd talk during the drive. I have some things to say."

"That's it? Just talking?" She sounded doubtful.

"And a kiss goodnight, if you'll agree."

"Aha."

"Just one. Then I'll leave."

Color bloomed in her cheeks. "I'm not sure I believe you."

"I give you my word." He dragged in another breath. "If I ever make love to you again, and I hope to God I will, I don't want a single doubt in your heart."

"You're confusing the heck out of me, CJ. I wonder if I know you at all."

"I want you to. I want to know you, too." He pressed her closer. The rounding of her belly was so slight that he wouldn't have noticed if he hadn't known.

The reality still scared him some, but it also made him so happy he wanted to shout the news to the world. "We made a baby, Iz. A person will come into being because of us. We need to get to know each other."

"I agree." Her soft smile made his chest hurt.

"Will you let me take you home? Please?"

"Yes."

He let out a breath. "Thank you." And the song ended.

"Wow. Perfect timing."

"I didn't plan it that way." Wrapping an arm around her shoulders, he guided her back to the booth where she'd tucked her purse under the seat.

"But you requested the song for our dance. Why?"

"It says some things about my feelings that I don't know how to say. Things that have nothing to do with sex."

"Oh, I think they have a little something to do with sex."

"All right." While she reached under the seat for her purse, he turned, located Matt and gave him a wave to signal they were leaving. "Maybe twenty percent is about sex."

She looped her purse strap over her shoulder. "How much of this evening did you plan?"

"Not much." Putting his hand at her back, he started toward the door. "I just knew I wanted to drive you home." The Brotherhood had taken it from there. "And not so we could make love, either. That was never my intention."

"*Never* your intention?"

He sighed. "I don't think I've realized how exacting you are." He held the door and ushered her through.

"I'm extremely exacting. It's one of the reasons my business got off the ground and has remained profitable."

"Then I'll be more specific, starting with last night. I slept with my phone under my pillow hoping you'd call and ask me to come over."

"I had no intention of doing that."

"I realized that eventually. Hey, it's chilly out here. Let's get you into the truck."

"I'm fine."

"You'll be more fine in the truck." He hurried her across the sidewalk, opened the passenger door and handed her in.

After he'd closed the door and come around to climb behind the wheel, he glanced at her. "Since you didn't call me during the night, I had to figure out when I'd see you next." He fastened his seatbelt and started the engine. "In the beginning, I imagined a group setting that would eventually become one-on-one."

"And we'd have sex tonight?"

"Yes, but then sometime during the morning, I—do I have to pinpoint the time?"

"No." Sounded like she was trying not to laugh.

"Okay. This morning I realized we're not ready to have sex."

"Sounds like you anticipate having it at some point, though."

"I wouldn't say I anticipate it. I'm... hopeful."

"Then you don't agree that it would be a mistake?"

"No."

"Because you're planning to move to Seattle?"

"Yes."

She groaned. "*CJ.*"

"But let's put that aside for now."

"I don't think I can when I know that's what you're working toward. Do you think making love again will convince me I can't live without you?"

"It's a possibility. My memory of that night is that we couldn't get enough of each other." Reminding her was part of his strategy, but it was a double-edged sword. His jeans pinched.

"Which is exactly why we shouldn't do it again. We'll both be better off if we can tamp down our urges."

"That's your opinion and you're entitled to it."

"Thanks." She folded her arms over her chest. Not a happy camper.

Well, neither was he. "Let me ask you something. When you called Friday and I responded with *I want to see you*, you seemed relieved and happy that we'd be getting together. Why was that?"

Silence.

"Izzy?"

"I was upset."

"Me, too."

"I was nervous about how you'd react. You might have been angry. Or disbelieving. You could have insisted I get another test to be sure."

"None of that crossed my mind. I was too busy scrambling for the right thing to say. From your reaction, it seemed like that's what you wanted to hear."

More silence. Then she took a shaky breath. "I did want to see you. I wanted you to hold me and tell me it would be okay, that we'd work this out." Her voice grew quiet. "I was only thinking of myself."

His chest tightened. Reaching over, he squeezed her shoulder. "We all do it. Nothing wrong with that."

"Maybe not, but until this moment, I didn't realize I'm responsible for this mess we're in. I shouldn't have come."

"What?"

"Over the weekend I started thinking of you for a change and I knew you'd want to make love this week. Shoot, I did, too! But—"

"Hang on." He slowed the truck as he entered the road leading to her cabin. "We're almost there. This is important. I don't want to be driving while we talk about it."

She took a shaky breath. "Okay."

"One thing you need to understand, though. If you hadn't chosen to come here, I would have been on a plane to Seattle. I was going to see you, Iz, come hell or high water."

12

CJ's declaration helped, but not much. Filled with self-recrimination, Isabel waited until he'd parked in front of her cabin and shut off the motor.

Then she unbuckled her seatbelt and turned to him. "Do you want to talk here or on the porch?"

He smiled. "Here is safer. The less time I spend on your porch the better." He swept a hand toward her. "You have the floor."

Such a good guy. Such a thorny problem. She cleared her throat. "When I realized sex would likely be part of my stay, I asked my doctor about whether it was a problem."

"So you said."

"She asked whether I was going to resume relations with the baby's father. She was delighted when I said yes. Clearly she liked the prospect of the relationship continuing. I finally saw that a week of lovemaking would be the start of an impossible affair."

His eyes glittered in the light from the porch. "Not if I move."

"I never expected you to suggest that. Which only shows how little I know you."

"If it makes you feel any better, I surprised myself with that decision, but I'm—"

"CJ, don't do it. I can't stop you, but please give up the idea. It's not the answer. If you don't believe me, ask Lucy. She grew up there. She wants to believe you could adapt, but she admitted it's a long shot."

His chest heaved. "She's probably right, but I've faced tough odds before."

"You wouldn't even be thinking this way if I'd stayed in Seattle instead of running down here to get comforted by you."

"And Lucy."

She nodded. "And Lucy. But mostly I came to be with you. Bad decision. If I hadn't—"

"I would've hopped a plane."

"And consequently been immersed in the city. You'd have faced the reality of noisy traffic, my tiny apartment and the frantic pace of my life as a business owner. I'm reasonably sure you wouldn't have considered moving there after that."

"But you don't know for sure."

"We'll never know, because I came here. I walked off that plane rehearsing my speech about living separate lives. Then you took me in your arms and my perfect solution has been unraveling ever since."

He reached for her hand and slid his fingers through hers. "It needed unraveling. Please don't beat yourself up over this. From my standpoint, you coming here was the best move."

"How can you say that?" The warmth of his touch radiated up her arm and spread through her body. *We couldn't get enough of each other.* She swallowed.

"This is where it all began." He stroked his thumb gently over her palm. "This is where we need to be while we tease out a solution."

"Is there a good one? If so, I can't see it."

"I can. We found something special back in April. I believe we could find it again. And I'm not talking about sex."

Her pulse rate climbed with every lazy stroke of his thumb. "Be honest."

"*Mostly* I'm not talking about sex. Like for example, I'd like to tag along on your ride with Matt and Lucy tomorrow. But I won't if you don't want me to."

"Of course I want you to. But I understand the dynamic better, now. What I want and what's best aren't the same things. After this discussion, I'm wondering if I should pack my bags."

He sucked in a breath. "I'd rather you didn't."

"But you've suggested rekindling the flame while I—"

"Oh, it's rekindled, Iz. I doubt we'll succeed in dousing it anytime soon, even if you hightail it out of here."

"You make it sound like I'd be running away."

"If the shoe fits."

"I'd be trying to make things easier for both of us."

"Speak for yourself. Your leaving won't make my life easier. Just the opposite."

The tension in his voice ramped up her frustration. "*I don't know what to do.*"

"You had a plan when you came. If you leave now, you won't satisfy one of your stated objectives."

"Which one?"

"That we become friends." He gazed at her. "You do still want that, right? To give us a better chance of getting along as we co-parent our baby?"

"That was my original goal."

"It's a good one, too."

"Are you saying you want to pursue a friendship with me?"

"That and more. I'd like to rediscover the connection we had during the wedding weekend, the mutual admiration society that led to climbing into bed the last night."

"Because you're hoping it'll lead us there again?"

He laughed. "Yes, ma'am. Can't blame me for that. But if friendship is all I get, that's the way the cookie crumbles. FYI, riding together promotes friendship. Ask anybody on the ranch."

"I'll take a wild guess that you've already mentioned this to Matt and Lucy."

"I have. It's fine with them, but you have veto power."

When it came to getting his way, CJ had skills. She'd be wise not to underestimate that as she navigated this tricky situation. But the prospect of seeing him on a horse was too delicious to pass up. "I'd like you to go. We can work on cultivating our friendship."

"Definitely." He gave her hand a squeeze. "I should let you go in. Get some rest."

"Good idea." She was wide awake and humming with sensual energy. Putting a closed door between this cowboy and her aroused self was a wise choice. Not her first one, though.

He released her hand. "I'll walk you to the door."

"That's not necess—"

"Yes, ma'am, it is. I still want to claim my kiss." He was out of the cab and around the front of the truck before she'd opened her door all the way.

To be fair, his last comment had distracted her. "What does a kiss have to do with friendship?"

"I'll be friendly about it." He helped her down.

If she had a brain in her head, she'd nix the kiss. But as her brain had taken a sudden vacay, she was totally looking forward to it. He was an excellent kisser. The brief touch of his lips when he'd met her at the airport had barely tapped into his abilities in that department.

"I've never given you a goodnight kiss."

"I guess not." She climbed the steps, her hand in his, her nerves vibrating in anticipation.

"Just a good-morning one."

Her breath caught. "No fair." Her core tightened.

"One of my favorite memories. You were so warm and relaxed."

"Well, I'm not relaxed, now." His lingering kisses from throat to thigh had led to the most intimate kiss of all, giving her one last orgasm. *To remember me by*, he'd murmured before slipping out of bed.

When they arrived at her cabin door, she turned to face him, heat simmering in her veins. "You're not kissing me." She freed her hand from his.

"Okay, I shouldn't have brought up the—"

"I'm kissing you." Lifting off his Stetson, she cupped the back of his head, rose to her toes and brushed her mouth over his.

He groaned softly. "Be my guest."

Lips parted, she pressed lightly at first, relishing the contours of a mouth designed for this activity. No prickle of scruff marred the sensuous connection. She drew back a fraction. "You shaved."

"Just for you, Iz." His warm breath caressed her lips as he enclosed her in his strong arms. "Don't stop."

"Not gonna." She took the kiss deeper, exploring with her tongue. His virile body tempted her to nestle closer.

With a hum of pleasure, he tugged her against his broad chest and aligned her hips with his. Uh-huh. Easy to tell what he had in mind.

Her body responded with a rush of moisture. She hadn't meant to whimper, though. The needy sound erupted on its own.

His grip tightened and the balance shifted. Fine with her. She loved it when he went all in.

He was there, now. When CJ funneled all his manly energy into kissing her, she ran up the white flag. He was devastatingly thorough, a smokin' hot cowboy in full command of his powers. He could have whatever he wanted.

She was at the point of dragging him inside when he slowed down long enough to lift his head. She tried to coax him back.

Gasping, he resisted. "No, Iz. I can't kiss you anymore. If I do, we'll be in your bed in five minutes."

"Yes, please." She struggled for breath.

"I promised we wouldn't."

"Some promises are made to be broken."

"Not this one." Slowly, with great tenderness, he released her. He made sure she didn't topple over as he took back his Stetson.

Good thing, because she wasn't all that steady on her pins. "I thought..." She pressed her hand to her heaving chest. "Didn't you say you wanted..."

"It's taking all I've got to back away." His hot gaze started the fire all over again. "But I could ruin everything."

"If I say it's fine, then—"

"You could wake up in the morning and remember my broken promise. You can't imagine how much I want to make love to you right now."

"Oh, yes, I can. It's written all over you." She glanced pointedly at the fly of his Wranglers. "Especially on the area below your belt."

"The kiss was my idea. I apologize for leaving you frustrated."

"And you're not?"

"Sure, but I expected to be. I made that bargain with myself because I couldn't stand going another night without kissing you. I wanted a real one, not the socially correct gesture in the airport."

"There was nothing socially correct about what happened just now."

"No." A slow, sexy smile appeared as he held her gaze. "Think of it as a preview of what we could have if we give ourselves a chance."

"So you're really not coming inside?"

He shook his head.

"I can't decide whether to admire your restraint or punch you in your sculpted abs."

"Goodnight, Izzy." He touched two fingers to the brim of his hat and walked back to his truck.

She stood on the porch until he drove away. Any minute he'd come back because he couldn't stand it. But he didn't come back. Which told her a great deal about Cornelius Jasper Andrews.

_13_

Should he take Izzy up on her offer? CJ gripped the wheel and forced himself to keep driving when every instinct screamed _turn around, idiot. You had her right where you wanted her._

Yeah, but he'd been fighting dirty. He'd brought up her last orgasm to find out if it was still as fresh and vivid for her as it was for him. In the soft, pre-dawn light, he'd been inspired to give her a goodbye gift.

Half-awake, her warm body relaxed and welcoming, she'd surrendered more completely than ever before. She'd been his to caress, to pleasure, to love. Then he'd left without taking anything for himself. He'd wanted their final connection to be all about her.

Noble? Hell, no. Selfish and prideful. He'd wanted to make a lasting impression, be better, more giving, than any guy before or since. He'd hoped she'd miss him. A lot. _Possessive much, cowboy?_

He hadn't accepted the restrictions on their relationship back then, even though he'd believed he had. His sperm hadn't accepted them, either. Those determined little swimmers had stormed the barricades to guarantee Izzy wouldn't forget CJ Andrews.

Rafe's truck was parked beside the bunkhouse, so the party must have broken up soon after he and Izzy left. When he opened the squeaky front door, the bunkroom was empty and a conversation was in progress in the kitchen. It abruptly ceased, which probably meant they were talking about him.

"Don't let me interrupt," he called out.

"Come join us for a cold one," Rafe said. "We want a report."

They deserved one, since they'd pitched in to help, but they didn't need every detail. He walked in, grabbed a bottle of cider from the fridge and took his usual seat at the kitchen table. "First off, thanks."

"Don't mention it." Nick grinned. "She and I bonded over the eating thing. Only problem was her tendency to talk about you all the time."

"No kidding." Rafe leaned back in his chair. "We were dancing pretty fast, but she still managed to get in some discussion of your Seattle plans. She's against them, in case you needed to be reminded of that."

"Yeah, no." He twisted the top off his cider. "I'm aware."

Garrett drained his bottle and set it on the table. "Since you're back so soon, I assume you stuck with your program and didn't go in."

"That's right."

"But he got some mouth-to-mouth action," Leo said. "Definitely some friction happened there."

CJ sighed and ducked his head. Some guys could kiss a woman for hours and their mouth never got red. His always did.

"I was trying to be polite and not mention it," Garrett said.

Rafe chuckled. "FYI, we're not that polite around here. If one of us comes into the bunkhouse with make-out mouth, we'll comment. Same deal if a shirt's buttoned wrong."

"And if you come home with your fly open," Nick said, "you'll never hear the end of it. Not that I know anything about that."

"You sure learned your lesson, though." Leo tipped his bottle in Nick's direction. "It hasn't happened since."

"How can it when my social life is a barren wasteland?"

"You should ask Eva out," Leo said. "Besides being good at cutting hair, she's cute and funny."

"And she's stuck on CJ." Nick turned to him. "You do know that, right? She'd go out with you in a heartbeat."

"Not interested."

"Not now, obviously, but—"

"We still haven't heard CJ's report." Rafe glanced at him. "Did you settle anything on the drive home? Is she okay with you going riding tomorrow?"

"She agreed to it. But she's blaming herself for handling things poorly by coming here. She says if I'd flown to Seattle, I'd have realized I couldn't live there. Moving would've been a non-starter."

Rafe nodded. "She could be right."

"I don't want her to be right, damn it. But when she keeps pushing me away, I ask myself if I'm doing her any favors by insisting on this idea." He took an angry swig of his cider.

"Uh-oh." Nick gazed at him. "Someone's going negative. Turn that frown upside down, cowboy."

"Is she pushing you away?" Rafe leaned forward and rested his arms on the table. "Your make-out mouth indicates the opposite."

"Oh, I turn her on. Our chemistry is hotter than ever. That doesn't mean she wants me with her in Seattle. She's convinced we should follow the paths we were on before this happened."

"But we launched the Brotherhood campaign to change her mind," Nick said. "I get her point about Seattle, but after spending time with her tonight, I want to see you two work something out. You're nuts about each other."

"Then why was she on the brink of packing her bags tonight?"

"She was thinking of you." Nick held his gaze. "You should have seen the way she watched you dancing with Henri. She wants what's best for you."

"And I want what's best for her. What if I'm not it?"

"It's too soon to tell, bro," Rafe said. "I agree with Nick that she's crazy about you. I say follow through with your plan to court her. See what happens. Don't call it before you give it a chance to work."

Nick pushed back his chair. "You might also want to order a pizza topped with anchovies and see if you could stomach it."

Rafe stared at him. "Nicholas? What the hell?"

"Get CJ to tell you about it. I'm off to bed. Barn duty in the morning."

* * *

By the next afternoon when Matt led the procession out the gate to the meadow trail beyond, gray clouds had blocked the sun and rain in the distance curtained off the mountains. CJ brought up the rear behind Izzy with Lucy in front of her.

The storm was moving their way. A few stray drops dampened his shirt. He doubted that would be the end of it. "I hope everybody's okay with getting wet," he called out.

"Won't bother me," Lucy said.

"Me, either." Izzy's hat and boots made her look like a cowgirl, but her posture in the saddle and her grip on the horn gave her away. She was game, though. She'd followed instructions and mostly groomed and saddled Lucky Ducky, the senior horse they'd all agreed would be the best bet for her first ride.

Matt turned in his saddle. "That's Seattle women for you." He rode Thunderbolt, the black stallion he'd bought more than a year ago to begin his dream of a breeding operation. The stallion was already earning his keep with stud fees.

"I do love rain," Lucy said. She was on Muffin, the buckskin barrel racer Ed had given her in April so she could improve her racing skills.

"I don't mind it." CJ guided Sundance through the gate and leaned down to close it behind them. "But I'm not crazy about mud." The big bay was his favorite horse in the stable.

"Mud's not so bad." Izzy was probably talking to him even though she was still facing forward. Good chance she didn't trust herself to turn in his direction.

"Try cleaning the barn floor after twenty horses have tracked in a ton of it."

She laughed. "Can't you teach them to wipe their feet?"

"Great idea. Hey, Matt, why didn't we think of that?" The rain grew more consistent, tapping lightly on the crown and brim of his Stetson.

"I'll get right on it, bro. We'll need that in place by this evening, looks like. How're you doing back there, Isabel?"

"Terrific! Lucy and I are ducks. Right, Luce?"

"Quack, quack."

Matt laughed. "Alrighty, then. Since it's only rain and not a thunderstorm, we'll press on."

"Please do. I'm starting to get the hang of this. How do I look from the back, CJ?" A hint of insecurity crept into her tone.

A rush of tenderness caught him by surprise. "You're doing fine. You'll have better balance if you tuck your elbows in, though."

"They call that chicken wings," Lucy said. "I was bad about that when I learned to ride."

"When you were what... four?" Izzy pressed her elbows to her sides.

"Six. That's when I started taking lessons from Henri."

"Lucy has more years of riding experience than I do," Matt said. "Or CJ."

"But not more time in the saddle." Lucy swiveled to glance at Izzy. "Two weeks every summer times twenty is less than a year of steady riding. They may have started later but they have me beat by a country mile."

"But now you're a barrel racer and we don't know how to do that," CJ said.

"I'm eager to see a demonstration." Izzy's elbows stuck out again but she pulled them back in. "My friend, the barrel racer. She showed me a couple videos on her phone while we had our hair done yesterday. I can't wait for the performance on Saturday night at the Founders Day thing."

"The Babes on Buckskins put on a show." He dreaded Saturday—the end of Izzy's stay.

"I'm sure I'll be blown away, especially because I know so little about riding. Speaking of that, if you have any pointers for me, CJ, shout 'em out."

"Happy to." Objectivity was tough to come by when she was adorably intent on her task. He wanted to give her a pass, tell her she was doing awesome. But her intensity had prompted her to clench her muscles. "It'll help if you loosen up."

"Can you be more specific?"

"Relax your thighs and your tush. Move with the horse." *Like you move with me when we're making love.* Couldn't very well say that.

"My instinct is to grip with my thighs so I don't fall off."

"I understand, but the more you let go and pick up the natural rhythm of your horse, the better it will feel." Same with lovemaking. He had a one-track mind today. Today? How about every day since she'd arrived? Every hour?

"How's that?"

He blinked. She'd done it. Her tempting bottom had settled nicely into the curve of the saddle and her thigh muscles were no longer rigid. She moved in sync with the gentle rocking of Lucky Ducky's gait.

Didn't take much to imagine her rocking in sync with him. He cleared his throat. "Excellent."

"Just following your directions. They're very... descriptive."

Was that amusement in her voice? Had she guessed where his mind had gone? "Glad to be of help."

"Okay, folks." Matt guided Thunder around so he faced them. Water dripped from the brim of his hat. "I don't mind a little rain, but if we don't start back we'll be soaked to the skin. We might end up that way even if we turn around now."

CJ dumped the water off his hat. "I'm with you, bro."

"Okay." Lucy smiled at her husband. "Not everybody is rain-toughened like Izzy and me."

Izzy pulled her shirt away from her breasts, which clung to them in a damp caress. "I suppose there's also the matter of decency. We can go back."

Matt nodded. "CJ, take us home."

"Will do." He wheeled Sundance in a circle and started down the increasingly muddy trail. The rain came down harder, discouraging conversation, but he didn't dare pick up the pace with Izzy so new at this.

"A ride in the rain!" she called out. "So appropriate!"

"Reminds me of a certain song!" he hollered back.

"Me, too!"

Her response warmed him. They had a special song he could reference and she picked up on it. He could build on that.

Nobody spoke again until they reached the barn. Unsaddling in a downpour wasn't a picnic, but they got it done. They returned the horses to the pasture and wiped down the tack.

"CJ, I'll give you and Isabel a ride," Matt said after they'd toweled off a little.

Izzy peered out the partially open barn door. "Believe it or not, it's letting up some. Thanks for the offer, but I'd rather walk back to my cabin."

CJ glanced at her. "Want some company?" He held his breath and waited for the answer.

She met his gaze. "Sure."

14

It could be the rain. Or the arousing sight of CJ in cowboy mode astride that big coffee-colored horse. Or his sexually charged examples while giving riding instructions. Or the hormones turned loose by the baby he'd helped create.

Whether Isabel blamed one factor or a combination of many, she couldn't hold out any longer. If she didn't make love to that cowboy soon, she'd combust.

Matt and Lucy exchanged a look. They'd likely guessed how that walk in the rain would end. Judging from the heat that flared in CJ's eyes, so did he.

Matt put a hand on CJ's shoulder. "I'll take your evening barn duty."

"Thanks, but I'll be there."

He would? Then again, maybe he'd walk her home, kiss her and leave. He was capable of it.

Matt frowned. "But—"

"I'll be there, bro." He glanced at her. "Ready?"

"Uh-huh." She thanked Lucy and Matt for the ride and stepped through the door into what had become a misty rain.

CJ followed. "It really has let up."

She turned to him. "When is barn duty?"

"About an hour from now." He took her hand, laced his fingers through hers and started off. "Is this a Seattle kind of rain?"

"Yep. Perfect for walking in."

"That I agree with. Especially since we're already wet."

"Yes, I am, CJ. Inside and out."

His grip tightened. "Don't tease me, Iz."

"I won't if you won't. Are you coming in this time? Or will you kiss me and leave for barn duty?"

"What do you want me to do?"

"Come in."

"I didn't bring a condom."

"As we discussed last time, we're both healthy. We only used them in April for..." She started laughing.

"Yeah, birth control. Ironic, huh?"

"I want you to make love to me. Please."

"There's not a doubt in your heart?"

She groaned. "Oh, I have a million doubts. If that's your requirement, then—"

"Ideally, yes. But after giving up the chance last night, I'd be a fool to turn you down a second time."

Okay. She let out a gusty sigh. "But you're not staying?"

"Depends on your definition. I'll leave to handle my job, but I'm off the clock at six. What happens after that is up to you."

"I want you to spend the night."

"Then I will."

Ahhh, the whole long night... top-drawer lovemaking... they'd need sustenance. "Come over at six-fifteen. I'll have food."

"I could pick up—"

"I'll do it. I'll go over to the buffet and use the to-go containers. Dinner will be waiting for you."

"Can I make it six-twenty, instead?"

"Why?"

"Gives me time to shower and shave."

"You don't mind eating a cold dinner, then?"

"No, but five minutes shouldn't—"

"If you walk through my door freshly shaved and showered, I'll be compelled to lick every inch of your manly self."

He gulped. "Better go for the cold cuts and salads, then."

"Good idea."

His pace quickened. "Can we move a little faster? I know this was supposed to be a romantic walk in the rain, but—"

"You'd prefer a romantic run in the rain?"

"Yes, ma'am."

"Then let's go, cowboy!" She started off, clamping her hat to her head as her boots splashed water and mud everywhere.

He kept pace with her, laughing as he displaced his share of water and mud. His share was much larger.

Running up the steps to her porch, she gasped for breath and surveyed the situation. "Nobody's around. Let's strip down." She laid her hat on the nearby Adirondack chair and toed off her boots as she reached for the hem of her shirt.

After pulling it over her head, she checked on CJ. He stood frozen in place, his chest heaving as he stared at her lacy black bra. "CJ! Strip! Nobody's here now, but any minute they—"

"Right." He blinked and started unbuttoning his shirt while continuing to watch her. "Got distracted."

"Faster, dude." Shivering in the cool air, she unfastened her jeans and struggled out of them. Wet, muddy denim was a challenge, especially with CJ's hot gaze ramping up her excitement.

"Are you taking off your undies?"

"No. They're wet, not muddy." She concentrated on stepping out of her jeans without transferring any mud to her legs. But one sock was muddy from toeing off her second boot. She pulled off the clean one and leaned over to roll down the other one.

CJ made a sound low in his throat.

Glancing up, she came eye-to-eye with him. She'd unintentionally mesmerized the poor guy with her cleavage. "You're falling behind." She said it gently, because his hypnotic state was sweet, really. Her focus drifted to his fly. "Better get out of those jeans before you break the zipper."

He swallowed. "I just... you have... cute little goosebumps... and your nipples... then you leaned over and..."

"You're adorable." Removing her sock, she left it with the pile of muddy clothes and reached for the doorknob. "Meet you inside."

He unbuckled his belt. "Be right there."

"Hope so. I'll be waiting." She went through the door. She left it open for him but stepped out of the line of sight.

Just in time, too. As she peeled off her wet bra and panties, the rumble of a truck announced someone was on the access road that wound past the cabins. The truck drew closer and a male voice called out *Have fun, bro! Don't do anything I wouldn't do!* Sounded like Jake.

"Leaves me plenty of room!" CJ yelled back.

She grinned. Jake wouldn't keep this incident to himself. Soon the entire staff would hear that CJ had been shucking his clothes on her front porch.

She barely had time to toss back the covers before he hurried through the door and closed it behind him. She climbed into bed and pulled the sheet and comforter over her chilled body. Propping her head on her hand, she flashed him a grin. "Was that Jake?"

"That was Jake." He shoved off his briefs.

Her grin faded in a rush of adrenaline and a sharp tug from her core. Judging from the angle of his cock, getting caught undressing on her porch hadn't dampened his ardor. Neither had the cool breeze that had given her goosebumps.

What a magnificently sculpted body. Was he more cut than he had been two months ago? She swallowed. "Have you been working out?"

He nodded. "Borrowed Nick's gear. Lifting weights helped me... accept a few things." He approached the bed.

Anticipation gave her the shakes. "We've n-never made love during the day."

"No, ma'am." He took a shaky breath. "The preview outside was nice, but... may I?" He reached for the covers.

"You may." His courtly attitude thrilled her. "I've changed a little, too."

"I wondered. When you leaned over, your bra seemed too small."

"I thought I was gaining weight."

"And sure enough, you are." Taking hold of both sheet and comforter, he drew them aside. "Ah, Izzy." He knelt beside the bed and laid his palm on her slightly rounded stomach, spreading his fingers. "I can barely tell."

"The baby is still very small."

"But powerful."

"How do you mean?"

He lifted his gaze to hers. "What else would have brought you back to me?"

"Ah."

"Look at you. So incredibly beautiful." Sliding his work-roughened hands up her ribcage, he cupped her breasts.

Those talented hands, calloused from ranch duties, could bring her to a fever pitch in minutes. He'd ruined her for city boys.

He massaged her breasts, squeezing gently. "I like you pregnant, Izzy. Turns me on."

"Kinda   turns   me   on,   too."
Understatement.

"You'll have to guide me, though, tell me what feels good."

"That."

"Are you tender?"

"No." She shivered. "Eager. I want to be touched."

"That I can do." He tossed the covers aside. "Scoot over."

She moved to the middle of the bed and turned on her side. "I want to touch you, too."

"Can't think of anything better." He climbed in and lay on his side facing her. Sliding a hand beneath her head, he wrapped his arm around her waist.

She mirrored him, cradling his head and stroking his broad back. This had been the way they'd started the first time they'd made love—lying face-to-face, bodies aligned, desire simmering as they gradually turned up the heat.

Holding her gaze, he pulled her in close, his chest a wall of muscle against the cushion of her breasts, his cock pressing against her damp thigh. His throat moved in a slow swallow. "Never thought I'd be here again." His voice was gruff with emotion.

"Me, either. Feels so good."

"Always did." He rubbed the small of her back. "Funny, but I thought I'd walk in and tackle you. Instead I want to take it slow, since we only have time for one round."

"Doesn't feel quite real, does it?"

"No." Leaning closer, he pressed his lips to her forehead. "I'd better not be dreaming this."

She sighed as he kissed her eyelids, then her cheeks. "If I am, it better be a good dream."

"The kind where you come?" He feathered a kiss over her lips.

"Yes, that kind."

"It'll be my pleasure." He gave her an open-mouthed kiss as he eased a hand between her thighs.

Heart thrumming, she shifted to give him access. He'd only had one night to learn what drove her wild, but he'd learned it well. His thick fingers slid in with ease and his thumb pressed on exactly the right spot.

He lifted his mouth from hers. "You're drenched."

"Told you."

His voice roughened as he deepened the caress. "Makes me feel like a million bucks, knowing you want me this much."

She dragged in air as her body clenched. "I tried not to want you."

"Why?"

"Because... it's inconvenient." She sucked in another breath.

"It's not inconvenient right now." He bore down. "Come for me, Izzy. Make this a good dream."

She dug her fingers into his back muscles, panting as he brought her closer... *there*. "*CJ*."

"I'm here. Let go."

Arching against his hand with a sharp cry, she welcomed the waves crashing over her, again and again, carrying away the stress of days, weeks without CJ. Gradually the powerful surges ebbed, leaving her languid and cleansed. She sank back to the bed, sighing with pleasure.

He nibbled on her mouth. "Good dream?"

"Excellent dream." She struggled for breath. "Got any more... like that?"

"Yes, ma'am. Time for you to lie back and get what's coming to you."

She flopped over, boneless but already wanting more. "I hope you mean...what I'm imagining."

"Let's find out." Levering his big body above her, he nudged her thighs apart and settled down, his weight on his forearms as he dropped his hips.

The blunt tip of his cock touched her quivering entrance and she gasped. "Whoa."

"Yeah. No latex. Can you handle it?"

"Are you kidding? I can't wait." She clutched his hips. "I've never—"

"That makes two of us." He pushed forward, squeezed his eyes shut and cursed softly.

"You don't like it?"

He opened his eyes. "I *love* it. Do you?"

"Yeah."

His gaze darkened. "It's so good it's too good."

"I can tell by your eyes."

"I'll hang out here for a little bit, get used to the sensation."

"I say go for it." She tightened her core muscles.

His breath caught. "If you do that I won't have a choice."

"Want that good dream?"

"You know I do, but can you—"

"You bet I can." She squeezed again.

"Okay, we're doing this." He drew back and pushed forward. "Wow."

Her thighs began to tremble. "Keep going."

"Can't help it." He began to stroke. Laughing with delight, he picked up the pace. "Damn, Izzy. *Damn*."

"Yeah." Excitement churned through her as she stayed with him, rising to meet each thrust and urging him on. She came first, loudly and with great joy.

He followed, his deep groan vibrating through his body as his cock pulsed unconstrained deep within her.

Resting his sweaty forehead on her shoulder, he fought for breath. "A-maz-ing."

"Uh-huh."

He lifted his head and gazed at her. "Rest up while I'm gone. We're going to do this a lot."

_15_

CJ dressed on the porch while Izzy leaned in the doorway wearing a Buckskin Ranch terry robe. She looked way too warm and tempting. But if he gave in to that temptation, he'd be late for barn duty.

He could ask her to step inside and close the door, but he appreciated her impulse to keep him company while he buttoned his damp shirt and leaned against the porch rail to pull on his socks.

"I hate seeing you put on those clammy wet clothes. Must feel awful."

"Goes with the job. We work outside and sometimes it rains. And snows." He puffed out his chest and struck a pose. "Cowboys deal with it."

"Okay, Dudley Do-Right. Don't tell me you're enjoying the effort it takes to zip your jeans."

"Truth be told, I'd rather be unzipping them." He glanced at her. "It's not easy to leave you, Iz. Especially when you're giving me that special look and I know you're naked under the robe."

"Want me to go inside?"

"I'd rather have you stay and torture me with the gleam in your eyes."

"I don't have a gleam."

"That's what you think. You have a gleam right this minute."

"Must be a reflection from the one in yours."

"That may be so, but I'll wager you're thinking about my package, especially while I'm working so hard on this damn zipper. Draws your attention to the significant area." He gave it one last tug. "Got it."

"I suppose you think I fantasize about—"

"I fantasize about your body." He buckled his belt and picked up his boots. "Why should you be any different?"

She laughed. "You're right. I'm not. I've thought about your body quite a bit over the past two months. Might be why I noticed you've put on some muscle since I left."

"Didn't expect I'd get a chance to show it off." Leaning against the porch rail, he tugged on his boots.

"To me, you mean. You must have intended to impress some other woman eventually."

"A few years ago you would've been right. I worked on my six-pack for that very purpose." He picked up his hat from the Adirondack chair and gazed at her. "This time my only goal was to forget you."

"Oh."

"You seem surprised."

"Surprised and sad." She pushed away from the doorjamb.

"So was I." He walked toward her. "I had a hell of a time getting over you. I drank a lot and listened to depressing country songs."

"You got drunk because of me?"

"A few times. Then Nick suggested lifting weights. Seemed like a better way to go."

She padded out on the porch, barefoot, and stroked his cheek. "I'm sorry."

"Wasn't your fault." He captured her hand and placed a kiss on her palm. "We'd established the ground rules. I'd agreed to them."

"Because you'd rather have something than nothing."

"Right." Releasing her hand, he cupped her shoulders but maintained his distance. No way he'd mess up her white robe. "It's still true. That thing about not making love until you had no doubts is out the window. I couldn't hold to it." His grip tightened. "I crave you, Izzy."

Her expression softened. "I crave you, too. I hated walking away in April."

"That helps."

"I wanted to believe you'd be fine. But you weren't."

"Were you?"

"No."

Relief pushed the breath from his lungs. "That's good to know. I mean, it's not, because I don't want you to be miserable, but if we're in the same boat, then—"

"It doesn't mean you should pull up stakes and move to Seattle."

"Do you have a better solution? Because I—" He stopped when she frowned and took a breath, readying herself for an argument. "You know what? We just made beautiful love to each other and this is a topic that could rain all over our parade."

"But it's important. We—"

"I know it is." Lifting her by the shoulders, he gave her a quick, forceful kiss. "I'll be back at six-twenty, ready for more of your sweet loving."

"But we need to talk about—"

"I'd be happy to ignore Seattle for the rest of the night, if it's all the same to you." Releasing her, he tipped his hat, spun around and clattered down the steps. He didn't want to have another argument about Seattle. Not after the most incredible sex of his life.

And look at that. The sun was out. While he'd been loving Izzy, the clouds had moved off and the late afternoon sun had begun drying the soaked earth. He liked rain. He'd be fine in Seattle, even if nobody else thought so.

He was early getting to the barn, but better that than being late with his shirt buttoned up wrong. Nick wasn't there yet, so he used the time to lay straw over the muddiest areas in front of the barn. Between the exercise and the warm sun, his clothes mostly dried.

Fetching a brush from the grooming tote in the tack room, he carried it outside and started working on the caked mud decorating his jeans. He even had some patches on his shirt. Made him smile. That wild dash for her cabin had been great.

The de-mudding was still in progress when Nick showed up. "Hey, Nick." He sent him a brief glance and kept brushing.

"I can see why you had to shuck your clothes on Isabel's porch." Nick grinned. "You're a disaster area. What'd you do, roll in the stuff?"

"Ran through the rain."

"And the mud, evidently. Not too smart."

"I know." He stomped his feet to shake off what he couldn't reach. Good enough. "Couldn't help it."

"Yeah, well, I guess I understand that, once you got the green light. What I don't understand is why you're here."

He looked up. "Same reason as you. I have barn duty."

"You could have texted one of us to cover for you."

"Matt offered. I didn't like the idea of him giving up time off so I could be with Izzy. Sets a bad precedent if I start shirking my duties."

"But won't you have a better chance of changing her mind if you're with her more?"

"Maybe."

"Then as part of the campaign, shouldn't we assist you in arranging that?"

"Not if it means dumping my responsibilities on the Brotherhood. She knows I work full-time."

"I see your point. You don't want to look desperate."

"Too late. She already knows I am. But just because I'm desperate doesn't mean I get to be selfish."

"I don't see it as selfish. It's helping out a brother."

"I appreciate that, but for now, I'll stick with my work assignments."

"Okay. You going back over there after this?"

"Yep. She asked me to."

"Hey, that's encouraging, right?"

"Guess so."

"I want things to work out for you guys." Nick shoved his hands in his pockets and rocked back on his heels. "Did you make some progress this afternoon?"

He laughed. "I have no idea how to answer that, bro." He gestured toward the barn. "Let's go get us some lead ropes and catch us some ponies."

<u>16</u>

Right after Isabel finished tucking food she'd brought from the buffet in an under-the-counter fridge, her phone played Naomi's ring tone. Not good. They'd talked this morning. No reason for her to call tonight unless there was a problem at the shop.

She glanced at the time. Ten minutes before CJ would knock on her door. She tapped the icon for the speaker option. "Hi, Naomi. I only have a few—"

"The roaster's dead. Fred just left. Drum is warped. No point in fixing it."

"*Damn* it." Her stomach churned. Their maintenance guy had been with them from the beginning. He'd helped them find that reconditioned roaster. If he could have repaired it, he would have.

"Yeah, and—"

"But you have enough inventory to buy us some time, right? This morning you said—"

"That was this morning. Turns out there's a techie convention starting today. The organizers fell in love with Cup of Cheer when they were location scouting and they're sending attendees here in droves."

She groaned. "Can you estimate when you'll run out?"

"At this rate, Friday afternoon. I have a possible solu—"

"Give me a minute. Let me think." She paced the small confines of the one-room cabin. Her five-year-plan had just gotten kicked out the door. So had her budget. "Grab the paperwork for the roaster I have tacked up on my wish list bulletin board."

"Already called them. They can't ship until next week."

She swore under her breath. "What about that company in California? I have their brochure bookmarked on my computer. They're more expensive but—"

"I already checked. They're backed up, too. But I have a lead on a roaster. Fred did an install for a guy in Bellingham who wants to sell his roaster."

"No. I gambled on this one, but at least I got a limited warranty from the dealer. Buying from a private party would be a nightmare. We—"

"Izzy, *this* is a nightmare. We need a roaster by Friday morning. Thursday night would be better. The guy has a year-old model at a very reasonable price. If I close the deal tonight—"

"Have you talked to him?"

"Of course I talked to him! If I give him a deposit, he'll hire a crew to load that sucker into a moving van and drive it down here tomorrow.

Fred will come over after it arrives and hook it up."

"What do you know about this Bellingham guy?"

"That he's my freaking knight in shining armor! And that Fred's set to head up there first thing tomorrow morning to confirm the roaster's in good shape."

That was some consolation. "But it's still used. Why's he selling it? What if it's defect—"

"Fred will check it out."

"You're talking about risking tens of thousands. No warranty, no—"

"Want me to close the shop when the coffee's gone?"

"No! But this—" She paused. "Hang on. CJ's at the door." She clicked off the speaker function before opening the door.

His happy smile faded. "What's wrong?"

"Roaster died. I'm on the phone with my sister. Come on in." She stepped away from the door and put the phone to her ear. "What does George think?" He was the third member of the managerial team, and the employee who'd been with her the longest, not counting Naomi.

"He's scared to death. Doesn't want to make a move without you here."

"Are you scared?"

"You bet, but I'm not paralyzed like George."

She took a deep breath. "That's good."

"Do you want the guy's phone number?"

"Yes, please."

"I'll text it to you as soon as I hang up. I'll also send the picture of the roaster that he sent me. It looks brand-new, Iz."

"He could do a bait and switch."

"I don't have to pay him until the roaster's operational, so he's taking a bigger risk than we are. And Fred says he's legit."

"Then send me the info. In any case, I'll also look at flights. I doubt I can get there any sooner than tomorrow night, but I'd like to be there when Fred hooks it—"

"Sis, don't do that."

"Why not? This is a major crisis. I need to be there."

"If we go through with this deal, it'll either work or it won't. You being here isn't going to change that."

"But—"

"I'm handling it. You could end up spending a lot of money to change your ticket and you'll also cut your time short with CJ. Or have you settled everything with him?"

"Not exactly."

"Then stay until Sunday morning, like you planned."

"I'll see how much the change fee is."

"Izzy, I can han—"

"Listen, I'd better call this guy. We may be forced to take a chance on him, but I'll feel better about it if I can ask a few questions. I'll text you after our conversation."

"Okay. Love you."

"Love you, too." She disconnected and turned to CJ.

He held his hat in his hand as if unsure whether he was supposed to stay. "You'll be looking at flights?"

"Yes, but first I need to talk with a guy who has a used roaster for sale. He's less than two hours away and offered to arrange the delivery."

"Do you want me to make myself scarce?"

"No, I just don't want you to be bored." Her phone pinged with the text from Naomi. "I don't know how long this will take."

"I can amuse myself." He glanced toward the small kitchen nook. "I see you picked up bread, so we must be having sandwiches."

"That was the idea, that we'd... but then Naomi called and—"

"How about if I put the sandwiches together now?"

She hesitated.

"I could be wrong, but I doubt you're in the mood for licking every inch of my body."

She gave him a rueful smile.

"I'll fix the sandwiches while you make your call and text Naomi. Then we'll eat and talk about what's going on."

"Okay. Thanks."

"My pleasure." Leaning over, he gave her a quick kiss. "If you need me, I'll be right over there." He pointed toward the kitchen nook.

"Like I'd forget."

"Like I'd let you." He winked and walked away.

The touch of his lips and the scent of his shaving lotion stirred the embers. Her phone pinged a second time, signaling the text was still waiting. With a sigh, she focused on the business at hand.

Bob Kennedy turned out to be a genial man who'd launched a coffee shop on a whim and then discovered how much work was involved. After a few minutes of conversation, she agreed with Naomi and Fred. The guy seemed honest. She agreed to the deal.

Spending a large amount of money with no return policy was risky, though. She pressed a hand against her stomach to calm the butterflies.

"You okay over there?"

She glanced up and met his concerned gaze. "I will be."

"Sandwiches are made."

"Let me text Naomi and I'll be right with you."

"I hunted around for drink options and—"

"Oh, right. I didn't think of that when I picked up the food. I could have grabbed you some hard cider. I have either non-alcoholic cider or I can make decaf coffee."

"I'm good with whatever you're having."

"Cider, please." She texted Naomi, who answered with *don't fly home* and a smiley face emoji. When she looked up from her phone, CJ had taken their plates and cider to the little table near the window. He'd found napkins, too.

Pulling out one of the chairs, he gestured to it. "Have a seat."

"Thank you for doing this." She laid her phone beside her plate as she slid onto her chair.

"Gonna check on flights?" He took his seat.

"I need to. I doubt I can get there before the roaster arrives, but I can at least be on hand when our maintenance guy hooks it up."

"And give Naomi moral support."

"That's my thought, even though she told me not to come. She said it would either work or it wouldn't."

"Sounds logical."

"It does, but she's never dealt with anything like this and George, who's normally fairly steady, is freaking out. The shop is my responsibility. I should be there." She waved toward his plate. "Please start. I want to see how much extra it will cost me, assuming there's even availability."

"I'll wait."

"No, really. I hate to make you—"

"I'll wait."

That tone meant she might as well save her breath, so she picked up her phone and got on the airline's website. It didn't take long to discover coach seats were gone. She could switch to business class and add that to the change fee. "Damn." She put down the phone.

"Expensive?"

"Yep. I have to let the sticker shock wear off." She put her napkin in her lap. "Let's eat." She picked up half of her sandwich and took a bite. "Mm."

"Good?"

She chewed and swallowed. "I got so involved in the roaster thing I forgot I was starving."

"Then I'm glad I went ahead with the sandwiches." He bit into his.

"Thanks for suggesting it. I didn't even think to ask you. If you'll pardon me, I have a sandwich to eat." She dived in.

He polished off half his sandwich and picked up his cider. "I'll bet you didn't think of asking me to drive you to Seattle, either."

She paused, the second half of her sandwich halfway to her mouth. "Drive me? I couldn't possibly—"

"I don't know if I could get the time off on such short notice, but if I can make arrangements with Henri and the Brotherhood, we could leave as soon as you're ready. You might get home in time to take that delivery yourself."

"I would never ask that of you." She returned her attention to her sandwich.

"My point exactly. I'm offering. Want me to call Henri?"

She shook her head, finished chewing and swallowed. "I'm not so desperate to get home that I'd put you through ten hours of night driving after you've worked a full day. I assume that's what you're suggesting."

"Yes, ma'am."

"And then what? Come straight back?"

"Might grab a couple hours of sleep first, but yeah, I'd need to get back. This is our busy season."

"It's an extremely generous offer and I'm touched, but I'm not taking it." She finished her sandwich.

"I'll leave it open, in case you change your mind. How much extra were you looking at for the flight?" He took a mouthful of cider.

She tapped the phone. The screen with the total came up and she turned it so he could see.

He swallowed so fast he almost choked. "Holy crap. Don't tell me you're considering that."

"I'd rather pay it than have you risk your life making the trip. I'd offer to share the driving, but I'm horrible at long drives, especially at night. I fall asleep."

"I don't. Neither do the other guys." He grinned. "You see, we're cowboys and cowboys—"

"Are insane. I get it." She put down her cider when her phone chimed with Naomi's ring. "Excuse me. I'd better take this." Pushing back her chair, she picked up the phone and stood. With the phone to her ear, she walked toward the kitchen nook. "Hey, sis."

"I checked the flight situation and you'd have to book in business class on top of the change fee."

"I know."

"I'm asking you not to come. That's a lot of money."

"We're spending a lot more than that on the roaster. I should be there to—"

"What, exactly? Hold my hand? I'm a big girl, Izzy. I can do this."

"I know, but—"

"You don't trust me to take care of it?"

"No! I trust you!"

"I don't think so. Flying back here at great expense proves it."

That stunned her. "Then..." She gulped and did a mental one-eighty. "Then I won't."

"Thank you." A gusty sigh came through the phone. "I'm damn proud of how I've reacted to this crisis."

"You should be. You've done a spectacular job." Too bad she'd questioned her sister's every move. Ugh. "I apologize for not acknowledging that. You came through in the clutch."

"Yes, I did. And by the way, I'm having the old roaster hauled off tonight after we close. Fred's going to stop by and make sure that goes okay."

"Right. Good thinking. Don't forget the service door has to come off."

"I remember."

"Give Fred a hug for me, too."

"I will. And I'll keep you in the loop tomorrow with texts. I'll call as soon as the truck shows up. I'll text you pictures."

"I'd appreciate that."

"But that's tomorrow."

"Getting the old roaster out is no piece of cake. The thing's heavy."

"It'll be fine. I hired the same guys who hauled it in. They know the drill. Is CJ still there or did you send him away?"

"He's here."

"I'm guessing you planned to spend some time together tonight."

"We did."

"Then please hang up and enjoy your evening. Don't give this another thought."

She smiled. "That's a tall order."

"Hey, if he's as cute and fun as he looked in the wedding photos, I'll bet he can make you forget your roaster problems."

17

CJ didn't try to eavesdrop, but it was a small space. If he'd correctly interpreted the conversation, Naomi had just done him a huge favor.

Izzy disconnected the call and came back to the table, phone in hand, her expression subdued.

He stood and helped her into her chair. "I heard some of that."

"Evidently if I'd insisted on flying back, she'd think I don't trust her to handle the crisis." She laid the phone beside her plate.

"Ah." He returned to his seat. "*Do* you trust her?"

She hesitated. "With most things, but this is huge."

"And Cup of Cheer is everything to you."

"Not *everything*, but it's my passion. My dream. That said, my relationship with Naomi is more important than the shop. Even though originally she told me not to come back, I thought in her heart she wanted me there for moral support. I was wrong. She sees this situation as a chance to prove to me that she's capable of handling a crisis."

"And prove it to herself?"

She nodded. "Probably, and that's even more important. I wouldn't knowingly do anything to undermine her confidence. She was my rock when I found out about the pregnancy last Friday. Our roles reversed. She started giving *me* advice. I loved that."

"She's been pregnant?"

"No, but she immersed herself in the subject. While I was busy obsessing about the emotional implications for you and me, she unearthed everything she could find about the joy of pregnancy and childbirth. Then she shared it with me."

"I wouldn't mind having some of that info."

"I'll text you the links. It's great stuff. Thanks to Naomi, I changed my focus from our less-than-perfect circumstances to the miracle of bringing a new life into the world."

He regarded her silently for a moment. "Sounds like she responded well in that crisis, too."

"Very true." She took a deep breath. "And I'm sure she'll handle this one just fine. Putting it out of my mind isn't easy, though."

"Tell you what." Shoving back his chair, he stacked the empty plates. "Let's take a walk."

"Where?"

"Down to the barn. Horses are a very calming bunch."

"I believe that. Especially Lucky Ducky. That horse is totally Zen."

He carried the plates into the kitchen nook. "Do you want to grab a jacket?"

"I don't think so. It was nice when I brought the food back from the dining hall."

He took his hat from the counter where he'd left it, started toward her and glanced at the phone in her hand. "Gonna take that?"

"Naomi might—"

"Really?"

"No, not really." She held up the phone. "My security blanket."

"I'd be happy to volunteer for that position."

She smiled and put the phone on the table. "You're hired."

"Thanks for the opportunity. Let's go." He ushered her out the door and took her hand as they descended the steps. "Moon's up." He pointed to the pale crescent in the fading light. "Waxing moon."

"I always liked that better than a waning moon."

"Me, too. Henri's fond of a new moon. She says it's the best time for starting something."

"What was the moon doing the night we made this baby?"

"Orbiting the Earth, as it does."

She rolled her eyes. "You know what I mean. Maybe it happened during a new moon. That would be cool."

"I'll look it up. Ever since finding out that Henri keeps track, I usually do, too. With the excitement of the wedding and meeting you, I stopped noticing."

"But you did this month?"

"Yes, ma'am. The new moon was on Sunday night, only hours before you flew in."

"Interesting. I've never paid a whole lot of attention to moon phases. Winters in Seattle are cloudy and often you can't see it. Or the sun, for that matter."

"I read that."

"When?"

"Last night, on my phone."

"I don't have to ask why you were researching Seattle." She blew out a breath. "I wish you'd realize that you'd be nuts to—"

"Whoa, there, Izzy. Could we table that for now?"

"Um, guess so."

Getting her to chill might not be so easy. He drew her to a halt. "Hear that?"

"What?"

"Crickets. The sound of summer."

"I know the chirping from movies, but we don't have them."

"Seattle doesn't have *crickets*?"

She shrugged. "Not that I've ever heard. And if you moved there, neither would you."

Damn, couldn't seem to stay away from the subject. He squeezed her hand and started off again. "I like them, but it's not a game changer."

"Sure seems like one. You sounded like a kid who was told the candy store was out of his favorite lollipops."

"It's a holdover from my indulgent childhood." He congratulated himself when she laughed. Exactly what he'd been going for.

"I'll bet one of the guys said that to you."

"Jake did, but the others picked it up." He scanned the area around the barn. Deserted, everyone tucked in for the night. Releasing her hand, he lifted the bar on the barn's double door and slid it back. "I'll take you and our baby over a million singing crickets."

She groaned. "CJ, you're biting off way more than—"

"After you." He swept an arm toward the opening. The soft glow of baseboard lights along the aisle provided a touch of romantic ambiance. "Feel all that peacefulness coming at you?"

"I do." She smiled at him and stepped inside. "Very quiet."

"Except for some munching. The slower eaters have a little supper left."

"And someone just nickered."

"Lucky Ducky. Hoping for a treat. Didn't think of that."

"We'll go see him, at least. You were right about the calm atmosphere." She wandered down the aisle toward Lucky Ducky's stall. "Not much mud. Did you get them to wipe their feet?"

"I laid down some straw in front of the barn. Kind of like a doormat."

"I didn't see it when we walked up."

"Nick and I hauled it away after they were all inside."

"See, I knew there had to be something like that to help deal with the problem." She leaned on the door to Lucky Ducky's stall. "Hey, buddy."

The bay made his way toward her and stuck his head over the stall door. The dim light barely allowed the white four-leaf clover marking on his forehead to show.

Izzy scratched behind his ears. "He looks sleepy."

"I'm sure he is. Most of them are. That's why it's a good place to chill out."

Evidently Lucky Ducky figured out no treats were forthcoming because he moseyed back to his hay net.

Izzy turned. "Are *you* sleepy?"

"No, ma'am." The shadows hid her expression, but that question had promise.

"Naomi said if you lived up to your image in the wedding shots, you should be able to make me forget my roaster problems."

Okay, then. "Is that a challenge?"

"Just repeating what my sister said." Her breathing picked up.

That Naomi. What a pal. "I just remembered. I want to show you something in the tack room." He took her hand and started back down the aisle.

"But I was just in there this afternoon. Has something changed?"

"I'm sure you didn't see this. Pretty amazing."

"If you're talking about your manly bits, I've seen them already. Just this afternoon, in fact."

He grinned. "That's not what I meant. But admit it, you were amazed."

"Don't put too much stock in that." Clearly she was trying not to laugh. "I don't get out much."

That cracked him up. Must have been contagious, because she lost it, too. Laughter and Izzy went great together.

He hurried her into the tack room, kicked the door shut and pulled her into his arms. "Prepare to be amazed."

Nobody kissed like Izzy. When she opened to him, when she moaned and thrust her tongue into his mouth, he was a goner. Her enthusiasm soon had him panting and fumbling with her clothes.

Tugging her shirt from the waistband of her jeans, he stopped kissing her long enough to pull it over her head. He tossed it on the nearest thing, one of the ranch saddles. Then he returned to the joys of her hot mouth.

She was into the program, too. Snaps popped in a rapid succession as she wrenched open his shirt and pushed it off his shoulders. She ran into trouble with the cuffs.

He let go of her long enough to unfasten them and toss the shirt on top of hers. A small nightlight provided limited visibility, but it looked like she'd arched her back and unhooked her bra. The overhead switch was within reach, but the glare of it didn't fit the mood.

He held out his hand. "Let me take it."

She gave him the flimsy bit of lace, warm from contract with her skin, and he added it to the pile of clothes.

Closing the gap between them, he lifted her to her toes and aligned the fly of his jeans with the juncture of her thighs. He ached, but it was a bearable ache, the kind that preceded really good sex.

She leaned into him, winding her arms around his neck and pressing her taut nipples against his hot skin, cushioning his pecs with her soft, plump breasts.

Moisture pooled in his mouth. "Grab onto my shoulders."

When she did, he filled his hands with her sweet tush and lifted her off the floor. "Wrap your—" He didn't need to finish the sentence. She gripped with her thighs and locked her ankles behind his back. Her tempting nipples quivered inches from his mouth.

He swallowed. "Can you—"

"Like this?" Her voice was low and sultry as she carefully let go of his shoulder, cradled her breast and leaned forward.

"Yes, ma'am." With a sigh of gratitude, he took what she offered, closing his lips over the pebbled tip and drawing it in, rolling it between his tongue and the roof of his mouth.

She dragged in a breath. "More."

Hollowing his cheeks, he sucked gently as tension built behind his fly.

Her thigh muscles tightened. "Mm...feels...nice." Her breath hitched. "Please keep...doing that."

Judging from her rapid breathing, he might be able to make her come. Wild. That hadn't been his goal, but it was, now. Heart pounding, he sucked harder. She moaned, pushing the damp seam of her jeans against his abs. He pushed back as he rhythmically squeezed her firm little bottom.

His cock swelled, wanting in on the action. His boys ached in protest.

"Can't... believe this." She gulped for air. "I've never...CJ...I'm...this is...*crazy*." And she came, muting her cries as she trembled in the grip of her climax.

He damn near joined her. Fighting the urge, he reestablished control. Slowly releasing her breast, he kissed her damp skin as she gulped for air.

He'd loved this barn from day one. Never brought a lady friend here, though. Tonight it was the right choice. Great place to fool around, distract Izzy from her worries... and maybe coax her to fall for a cowboy.

18

CJ supported Isabel's weight as if holding her was no big deal, but he had to be getting tired. She finally had enough breath to speak without gasping. "That was awesome. You can put me down, though."

"Was it amazing?"

"Sure was." She dragged in more air. "Please put me down."

"I don't wanna."

"Your arms must be ready to fall off."

"Nah. I trained for this."

"For tack-room sex?"

"For whenever weight-lifting is required. Turned out it came in handy tonight. Since I can bench-press two-fifty, I—"

"Hey, I don't weigh *that* much!"

"Agreed. That's why I can easily hold your feather-light self for hours, but since we need a change of position for the next round—"

"Next round? Here?"

"Yes, ma'am. Afraid I can't wait until we get back to the cabin."

That comment made her shiver with anticipation. Nothing like a desperate CJ to fire her up.

"Izzy? You cold?"

"No. Excited."

"I like hearing that. Let me find you a nice spot." He carried her over to one of the sawhorses and perched her sideways on a saddle.

She grabbed the saddle horn and the curved back part...the...oh, yeah. *Pommel.* "Whose is this?"

"Basically mine." He dropped to his knees in front of her. "It fits Sundance and he's the horse I ride most of the time." He untied her gym shoes and took them off, along with her socks.

A simple gesture. Yet the care he took was typical CJ. "I could've taken off—"

"I wanted to. I like undressing you. Gives me an excuse to touch you." He held her foot in both hands and stroked the sole with his thumbs.

"Mm."

"Like that?"

"I like it all. You have great hands."

Leaning down, he ran his tongue between her toes. "Think I could make you come playing with your feet?"

The suggestion sent a ripple through her core. "I...maybe. Pregnancy seems to have turned my whole body into an erogenous zone."

"Can't wait to test that theory." He stood. "Let's get you out of those jeans."

"I'll stand up." She started to slide off the saddle.

He stopped her mid-slide his hands spanning her waist. "Not letting your bare tootsies touch this dusty floor."

"Then hold me right here." While he kept her in mid-air, she unfastened her jeans and shoved them, along with her panties, over her hips.

"Perfect." He lowered her back to the saddle.

The smooth leather under her bare bottom was sensual as hell. His commonplace suggestion of *let's take a walk* had turned into an erotic adventure.

He tugged off her jeans and panties and left to put them...somewhere. Shadows obscured most of the room's details. Shedding inhibitions was easy in a dark room filled by the scent of oiled leather and an aroused CJ.

The rustle of denim, a boot heel hitting the wooden floor and then another told her he was taking off the rest of his clothes. The rasp of a zipper was followed by a quickly stifled groan.

"Are you in pain?"

"Worth it." A floorboard creaked as he returned to her. "Worth every aching second to discover another way to make you come." His indistinct form became more defined as he drew closer.

Oh, yes, his manly bits were amazing. Heat sluiced through her. No wonder he'd given her a child. Virility like his would not be denied.

"Never tried this before." His breath hitched. "Guess you inspire me, Izzy. Grab hold of that saddle." He stepped between her knees and cradled her hips in his large hands. His cock easily found its way to the entrance of her snug channel. "Stop me if something...if it doesn't feel right."

Her heartbeat thundered in her ears as the intense friction set off tiny explosions, early storm warnings of the tempest that would soon sweep her away. The sensation of being filled stole her breath. "Feels...great."

He eased forward. "I want to be careful. Careful of our baby."

"She's fine."

He paused. "She?"

Had she said that? "Oh. I—"

"We're having a little girl?" Wonder laced his words. "I thought you didn't—"

"It's only a feeling."

"That counts." His breathing roughened as he tightened his hold and sank all the way in. He muttered in frustration. "Hold still. Very still."

Gripping the saddle, she worked to calm her eager body. The first spasm arrived, anyway.

His breath hissed through his clenched teeth.

"Sorry. Can't help it."

"Me, either. So good." He gasped again. "Hang on." He drew back and thrust home. "Next time...we'll take longer...make it last..."

She gulped. "Just love me."

"Yes...ma'am..." He held her steady and stroked faster.

Her core tightened. "Now, CJ...*now*." Her world exploded. Somehow she kept from yelling as wave after wave crashed over her.

He kept going, his rapid thrusts intensifying the pleasure, his voice hoarse as he called her name. At last he took what he needed, shuddering and gasping as the steady pulse of his climax created a last intimate caress.

Closing her eyes, she savored the energy of this vibrant man, his cock buried deep in her body, his muscled pecs heaving inches from her breasts, his warm breath teasing her nipples. His magnetic personality had pulled her in from the moment his gaze had locked with hers on a cool April evening eight weeks ago.

A connection that hot should have cooled just as quickly, right? Instead, their passion burned with a white-hot flame, melting the barriers between them, incinerating common sense. When he made love to her, she never wanted him to stop.

Leaning forward, he landed a kiss on her nose, chuckled and recalibrated, settling his mouth over hers. His supple lips delivered a relaxed kiss rich with shared satisfaction.

He hummed low in his throat and lifted his head. "That was the best yet."

"Uh-huh."

Holding her steady, he eased his cock free. "At the risk of sounding boring, I suggest we take this program back to the cabin and a soft bed."

"Doesn't sound boring to me."

"Good. Will you be okay for a sec while I fetch your clothes?"

"Sure."

He returned with her shirt and bra over his shoulder and her jeans and panties in his hands. Putting them on was easier than taking them off. She used the saddle horn and pommel to lift away from the saddle while he slid on her panties and then her jeans. Once he'd put on her socks and shoes, she could stand and get her jeans zipped and buttoned herself.

But he insisted on helping her with her bra. Slipping the straps over her shoulders, he reached behind her and fastened the catch. "I might be developing an obsession with your breasts."

"Fine with me."

He traced the top edge of a lace cup that was no longer adequate to the job. "That's abundance, right there." With a sigh, he backed away. "So tempting. But it's getting late. Pregnant ladies need their sleep."

"How do you know?"

"Read it, and Sarah told me, too." He quickly pulled on his clothes. "When she was pregnant with Amy, she needed lots of sleep. I don't want to wear you out."

"I'm okay." She swallowed a yawn. And smothered a second one.

CJ was intent on getting dressed, thank goodness. He was just the type to call a halt to their activities if he caught her yawning. Sleep was the last thing on her mind as they walked through the cool night toward her cabin.

"I hope you're right that we'll have a girl." He laced his fingers through hers. "I'd be excited about a boy, too, but I was really taken with little Amy."

"I'd be happy with either, too, but for some reason I think this baby's a girl."

"Sure you don't want to find out beforehand?"

She hesitated. "I'll think about it some more." His eagerness pushed her in that direction. She loved putting a sparkle in his gray eyes. Except...oh, yeah. She wouldn't see his reaction to the news unless he moved to Seattle.

19

Izzy was done in. CJ had caught her smothering a yawn twice on the way back to the cabin. When they arrived, she grabbed what looked like a nightgown from a drawer and disappeared into the bathroom.

He used the time to finish clearing the table. After closing the curtains over the front window, he doused all the lights except a lamp beside the bed.

Then he began stripping down, but not so he could seduce her. She needed sleep more than lovemaking. He'd convince her of that.

He'd ditched his shirt, boots and socks by the time she came out wearing a filmy little black number with a plunging neckline and a hem that stopped several inches above her knees. No fair. His package immediately took note of her outfit and responded with enthusiasm.

She made a slow turn. "Like it?"

"Yes, ma'am." He cleared the hoarseness from his throat. "But when you arrived, you said we shouldn't have sex. Why'd you pack that?"

She had the decency to blush. "I almost didn't. But—"

"You were secretly hoping I'd change your mind?" He walked toward her. "And then you'd have this to wear for me?"

"Probably. Oh, CJ, I was in such a state when I packed to come here asking myself *should we? Shouldn't we?* This nightgown went in last. I took it out a dozen times. In the end, it made the trip. On the flight here, I came to a decision—sex would be a mistake."

"Yet here we are." He reached out and drew her, seductive outfit and all, into his arms. "When did you get this?"

"About a year ago, after a breakup. I promised myself that someday I'd find a man who would appreciate it. And me."

"Did you?" If she'd worn this for someone else...

"I did."

He held his breath.

She gazed up at him. "That man is you."

"Damn, Izzy." He pulled her in tight. "I'd planned to suggest we get some sleep."

"And let this nightgown go to waste on its first outing?"

"You've been yawning like crazy." The silky material rubbed against his bare chest. It shifted over her cleavage. If he reached beneath that material, he'd—

"Please make love to me while I'm wearing this. That's all I ask."

"You want to leave it on?"

"Yes. It's part of my fantasy. Blind with lust, you won't bother to take it off, just shove it aside and ravish me."

"Ravish you? I can't be rough, Iz. The baby—"

"You don't have to be rough." Wiggling out of his arms, she moved over to the bed, pulled back the covers and climbed in. "Just slightly...untamed."

"Untamed." He ran his fingers through his hair. "I'm not sure what—"

"Aren't you the guy who made love to me while I sat naked on your saddle?"

"Yes, ma'am."

"Take off your jeans, cowboy." She stretched out on her side and her breast threatened to slip free of the nightgown's minimal restraint. "Come ravish me."

A switch flipped. The concerned father-to-be stepped aside to make way for the primitive mate she craved. Dispensing with his jeans and briefs, he crawled into bed fully aroused and focused. Didn't take much to awaken those instincts.

From the beginning, she'd had forever written all over her. One night stand? A wedding weekend fling? Bull. She was the woman he'd waited for and he was the man she needed. The baby they'd conceived proved it.

A hand at her shoulder, her pushed her to her back—not shoving, just taking charge. Moving over her, he yanked down the top of her outfit, exposing her lush breasts. And oh, how he feasted, satisfying the needs of his hungry mouth with nipping, licking and sucking all that bounty until she writhed and panted beneath him.

Bunching the nightgown at her waist, he reaching between her thighs and made her come, and come hard. She was still in the grip of her orgasm when he plunged his cock into her undulating channel.

Bending her knees back, he created a rhythm and an angle guaranteed to make her come again. When she did, he slowed the pace, settled onto his braced forearms, and took stock.

Her nightgown had become no more than a sash gathered at her waist. Technically she still wore it, but it was useless as a covering.

Flushed and breathless, she met his gaze.

He continued to stroke as her body gradually quieted. "Ravished, yet?"

Her breath hitched. "Thoroughly."

"That was fun." He smiled. "We'll have to do it again sometime." He glanced at the wadded-up material. "Unless I've ruined your—"

"It's sturdy material."

"Good, because I like it."

"You didn't come."

"Not yet. I had to finish the ravishing. Takes concentration."

"You did a great job."

"Figured that. You made a lot of noise."

"Did I?"

"Seemed like a good sign that you were loud. FYI, I won't hold you to any of those promises you made."

"Promises?"

"When you were coming the first time. And the second, too, now that I think about it. You promised to have sex with me whenever and wherever I wanted."

"You're making that up."

"Like I said, I won't hold you to it."

She stroked his sweaty back and slid her hands down to his glutes. "You can for the next three days."

Sobering. Three days wasn't much time. "Then I will." Leaning down, he kissed her to seal the deal. But lots of sex might not be enough to persuade her he was the one. He'd have to come up with more than that.

For now, he'd work with what he had. Disengaging from her sweet body, he grabbed a pillow from the far side of the bed. "Lift your hips." He tucked the pillow under her and returned his needy cock to its happy place.

Her breath caught. "Nice."

"I hoped you'd like it. You're welcome to grab my ass again."

She took him up on that suggestion. "Turns me on to feel your muscles working."

"Good." His gaze locked with hers as he moved deliberately, stroking her G-spot, making each thrust count. "Ravishing's over."

"I know." Her voice was soft. "We're making love."

"Yes, ma'am." He kept the pace steady, letting her catch up while he held back.

Then she was there. Her eyes darkened and her fingers dug in, pulling him deeper, rising to meet him, gasping his name. Sweet, sweet sound.

When she cried out, he buried his cock to the hilt in her quivering channel and let go. His ears rang as the pulsing of his release merged with hers.

Beautiful.

20

Isabel woke when the door to her cabin clicked shut. She jumped out of bed, the black nightgown still wrapped around her waist. Couldn't go to the door like that.

As she wrestled with the slippery material, CJ crossed the porch and descended the steps, his footsteps light for such a big guy. She hurried to the window and moved the curtain to peek out. Maybe he'd look back and she could get his attention.

Nope. His ground-eating strides took him rapidly away from her. He followed the curve of the access road. Gone.

With a sigh of regret, she let go of the curtain, pulled off her nightgown and headed for the shower. He must have taken great care not to wake her when he'd left the bed and dressed. Evidently he valued her sleep over telling her goodbye.

Next time she saw him she'd let him know she preferred a goodbye, and maybe a kiss to go with it. His choice was understandable after Sarah had advised him about the sleep needs of pregnant women. But this situation wasn't anything like Sarah and John's. They lived together and saw each other constantly.

She and CJ had to create a plan for getting together. Because he'd left without waking her, they didn't have one. What was his work schedule? When was his lunch hour? Did he get breaks during...wait, what was she doing?

Swearing softly, she derailed the crazy train and stepped under the welcome spray of a hot shower. Her frantic desire to see him didn't bode well for her long-distance parenting decision. She needed to calm the hell down.

Besides, he hadn't hopped a plane to Paris. He lived on this ranch. He had a cell phone. She had one, too. They could discuss the day's activities via text.

And speaking of her cell phone, she might want to charge it because—guess what?—she had a roaster issue going on in Seattle. Why hadn't she focused on *that* first thing this morning?

Naomi had been right about CJ. He'd totally distracted her. Connecting with him had been her top priority when she'd opened her eyes.

Quickly finishing her shower, she blotted her damp hair with the towel before wrapping it around her and padding back to the table by the front window. She'd put her phone on it before going to the barn with CJ.

It was still there. She'd gone right past it, oblivious, desperate to catch CJ before he left. She picked it up. No messages from Naomi on the screen. But a message was scrawled on the Buckskin Ranch memo pad lying under the phone. *Text me when you wake up.*

Aww. Warmth flooded her chest with an emotion she'd rather not name. He hadn't just left, after all. He'd wanted to hear from her first thing and probably had assumed she'd reach for her phone before she did anything else. Normally, especially with the roaster situation, she would have.

Securing the towel in place, she typed quickly. *I'm awake. Sorry I missed you.*

Instead of texting, he called. "Hey." His soft greeting created an intimacy that arrowed straight to her core.

"Hey, yourself. I thought you'd text me." And why was her heart pounding so hard?

"Wanted to hear your voice."

Her breath caught. "Where are you?"

"Just got out of the shower."

"Funny, so did I."

"You showered before texting me?"

"I didn't see your note until a few seconds ago."

"You took a shower before checking your phone?"

"Shocking, I know. Not like me at all."

"Guess you weren't thinking about your roaster issue, then." He sounded pleased with himself.

"Nope."

"Any word from Naomi?"

"Not yet. I'll assume everything's fine."

"Good plan." He hesitated. "Did you think about me when you were in the shower?"

"Yes, but not the way you're imagining."

"How do you know what I'm imagining?"

"I can hear it in your voice."

His sexy chuckle tickled every nerve ending in her body. "Bet you can. Hey, Jake and I are going out to the raptor center site during our lunch break so he can fill me in on the plans. He's making sandwiches to take along. He'll make one for you if you'd like to go."

"Love to. On horseback?"

"In my truck. Just a quick trip."

"Is it okay if I bring my phone? I'll silence it, but—"

"By all means bring it. Wouldn't want you to miss hearing from Naomi."

"I appreciate that. I'm excited to see the site, though, after hearing about the plans. Thanks for thinking of me."

"I can't stop thinking about you...the way you looked when I left, snuggled under the covers fast asleep, your hair mussed from making love." His voice grew husky. "Wasn't easy to leave."

"I heard the door close and jumped out of bed, but I wasn't fast enough to catch you."

"Just as well. If you had, I would've been late to work."

"But I wanted to tell you goodbye."

"And I would have kissed you and after that...it'd be all over."

"Then maybe we need to set an alarm. Make it early enough to give us a little time before you leave."

His breath hissed. "You've got it. Now I'm getting off this phone before one of the guys notices my condition. Jake and I will come by the cabin a little after twelve."

"I'll be ready."

"'Bye, Iz."

"'Bye." She disconnected and went in search of her charger. His phone call sure had juiced her batteries. Going out to the site of the future raptor center would be fun. But she might as well not kid herself. The main attraction was CJ.

* * *

Isabel was on her way out the door to get breakfast at the dining hall when Naomi called. Ducking back inside the cabin, she closed the door and answered the phone. "What's happening?"

"First off, last night went perfectly. The old roaster's gone." Noise from the shop filtered through the closed office door.

"Good. Sounds busy out there."

"Crazy busy. It's all-hands-on-deck time. Anyway, I just talked to Bob. The movers are running late. Should be there in another half-hour or so. He has no clue how long it'll take to load the roaster and secure it before they start down here. He's never done this and neither have they."

"That's not very reassuring."

"I almost didn't tell you, but I promised complete transparency, so—"

"Thanks. Please keep me in the loop."

"Like I said, I promised, so I will, no matter if the news is good or bad."

"It'll go smooth as silk."

"Yes, it will. Was CJ a good distraction?"

"Uh, you could say that."

"I think it's so cool that you dig the father of your child."

"I guess it is, at that."

"Are you going riding again today?"

"Nope, but I get to check out the site of a raptor rescue center that'll be built on the ranch this summer."

"Awesome! Remember the eagle's nest cam we used to watch as kids?"

"Yep. I loved that. Hey, I don't want to keep you. You said it's crazy and—"

"It is, but I also like hearing what's going on with you. Are you having a good time?"

She blinked. "I...guess I am. Why?"

"You seem more relaxed."

"Yeah, I really want to apologize for yesterday. When you called about the roaster, I was—"

"I don't mean more relaxed than you were yesterday. I mean relaxed in general."

"You can tell that over the phone?"

"Your voice is different, more like it used to be."

"When?"

"Before you opened the shop. I get why it changed. The shop is a huge responsibility. But now you sound more like yourself again."

She laughed. "I have no idea what you're talking about."

"Just take my word for it. Maybe it's the atmosphere of the ranch, or getting to spend time with Lucy. But my money's on CJ. I think he's good for you, sis."

21

"Seems like old times, Jake." CJ tore up lettuce, sliced tomatoes and cored avocados while Jake assembled the sandwiches. "You and me fixing food in the bunkhouse."

"It'll be old times all over again for chuck wagon stew tomorrow night, unless you and Isabel are ditching us."

"I figured we'd be there, but I forgot to mention it to her. I'm sure she'll want to come, though, especially now that we've set up a table out by the fire pit."

"That area's worked out great. If we end up deciding to initiate Garrett into the Brotherhood, I want to do it out there." He wrapped another sandwich and tucked it into the cooler. "Don't know if you've heard, but the Babes' shower for Isabel is a definite for tonight."

"Hadn't heard that." Henri had told him it was in the works when she'd come down to the barn this morning. Having the ladies give Izzy a party was a nice idea, although he'd pouted a bit about losing precious time with her.

"Isabel didn't text you?"

"Haven't heard a peep from her since early this morning. She's probably busy getting updates about her roaster." He sliced the last tomato. "That shower came together fast."

"It's now or never for the Babes."

"I get that." He rinsed off the cutting board and the knife. "I'm worried about their plan to brag on me, though. I told Henri it could backfire."

"You don't think some five-star reviews from the Babes could help your cause?"

"Not if they overdo it."

"Let's see how lunch goes. If she seems totally smitten during our picnic, then maybe you don't need those reviews."

He sighed. "I need time, not promotion. I wish I had another week."

"Could you ask her to stay longer, offer to pay for changing her ticket?"

"That wouldn't go well." He grabbed an unopened bag of chips from the cupboard. "She's worried about her shop. If her sister hadn't stepped up, Izzy would already be on a plane."

"Okay, forget that idea." Jake tucked three bottles of apple cider in the cooler. "Assuming she goes along with your move to Seattle, what's your timeframe?"

"End of summer, early fall. I'm not leaving Henri in the lurch during our busy time. If she finds a replacement and he works out well enough that I could take off, then I might go earlier."

"Seems like you've thought this through." He added paper plates and napkins to the cooler and closed the lid.

"I have. Gotta make it work. Somehow."

Sadness flickered in Jake's eyes. "Still haven't quite grasped it, bro. When Seth moved, he was less than four hours away and in the same state. For some reason that made it less dire. But you...."

"It won't be easy. But you'd do the same in my shoes."

"Yeah. Glad I don't have to, though. I've told Millie so many times that I'm grateful she wants to stay here. I feel like I should vet everybody's girlfriend from now on. I can't lose anybody else." He picked up the cooler and started out of the kitchen.

"Did you ever think of sabotaging this relationship instead of promoting it?"

He glanced over his shoulder. "For about two seconds. Then I heard Charley's voice in my head." He headed for the front door.

"I hear that voice all the time, too." CJ grabbed his keys and the bag of chips and followed him out the door. "That's why I'm determined to make this happen."

"Understood." Jake put the cooler in the back seat but rode shotgun on the way over. Then he transferred to the back when CJ climbed out to fetch Izzy.

She opened the door before he made it to the porch. Her red T-shirt had *Apple Grove* stenciled across the front. Combined with her hat and boots, she could almost pass for a local. Just needed more wear on those boots.

He smiled. "Looking like a cowgirl, Iz."

"Thanks." She crossed the porch and came down the steps.

"What's going on with the shop?"

"Old roaster's gone, new roaster's on its way. Did you know about the baby shower?"

"Just heard about it this morning, after I talked to you."

She paused when she was only a couple of feet away, as if she wanted to talk privately before heading to the truck. "It's so thoughtful of them. But like I told Lucy, it feels strange since I've only known about the baby for a week."

"They want to give you stuff in person." He nudged back his hat. "I get that."

"Me, too." She lowered her voice. "Guess we won't have dinner together, though."

"No, ma'am."

"Do you still want to—"

"Yes, ma'am."

She grinned. "You don't know what I was going to ask."

"Yes, I do." Anticipation played hell with his breathing. "Mind if I bring a duffle over with a change of clothes and my shaving kit?"

"Not at all." She fingered a button on his shirt. "I'll leave the door unlocked. Come over and make yourself at home."

The invitation sparkling in her eyes made his heart pound. "Best offer I've had today."

"I don't know how long the party will last. Since I'm the guest of honor, I can't exactly leave early."

"I understand." While she was otherwise occupied he could add some romantic touches to the cabin. This could work out. "I don't mind waiting." He gestured toward the truck. "Ready?"

"Sure am." She winked at him and headed for the truck. "Where's Jake?"

"In the back. He vacated the front seat expressly for you."

"Nice. I'm becoming fond of cowboy manners."

"I'm glad. Gives me an edge."

"Like you need one."

"Oh, I do, Izzy. I definitely do." He handed her in and she turned to thank Jake for giving her the front. By the time CJ rounded the hood of the truck and climbed behind the wheel, she and Jake were involved in an animated discussion about the raptor center.

"We have stakes in the ground," Jake said. "The contractor came out yesterday."

"He did?" CJ turned back to him. "You didn't tell me."

"You didn't ask."

"Didn't think to. What else haven't you mentioned?"

Izzy answered for him. "Jake's started building the enclosures for the birds. Today we're going to help him map out a possible pathway and potential locations for each one."

"Sounds great." CJ started the engine and pulled out. "But that's a major assignment, bro. Do we have time to eat these sandwiches?"

"Plenty of time. I've already marked a preliminary route. I just need more input. I want you to pretend you're a visitor to the center. Tell me whether my chosen path is the most logical."

"That'll be fun." CJ took the ranch road back to the two-lane, made a left and went about three hundred yards to a newly created dirt road. By the time visitors used it, the road would be paved and have signage to offer directions. "Did you consult with Zane?"

"I've been videoconferencing with him."

"Yeah?" Impressive. His buddy seemed to be moving smoothly into this role. "Did he have advice on the pathway?"

"Some, but he didn't have enough time to work any of that out when he was here on Monday. We were focused on the preliminary plans for the building and where to put it. The pathway and enclosures will be my job. Henri's overseeing the visitor center construction."

Izzy swiveled to face Jake. "Which will come first, the visitor center or the enclosures for the birds?"

"I'll get the enclosures finished before the center. Ideally we won't have anybody bringing us birds right away, though. Construction noise could be an issue. Zane had birds long before he and Mandy decided to build a visitor center, so he draped the enclosures with burlap. He said that helped."

"Do you have a vet lined up?" CJ guided his truck carefully over the new road. Yesterday's rain had added some ruts.

"Evan gave me a name." He glanced at Izzy. "Evan's our equine vet. He knows someone who might be interested. We've been playing phone tag so I haven't talked to her, yet."

"Lining up the right people for a new project is like putting together a puzzle," Izzy said. "At least it was for me with the coffee shop."

"I can see that. Although I've never done anything remotely like this before. I had to put a day planner app on my phone."

"It can be intimidating, but each step brings you closer to your vision for it. Just imagine how it'll grow in the next year, five years, ten, twenty...."

"Excellent point. I never used to think that way. Just lived day-to-day. Being with Millie's changed that."

"Being with Millie has changed a lot of things for you, bro." The road ended and CJ pulled into the clearing designated for the raptor center.

"Yeah, it has. But visualizing a future, specifically with her, was the game-changer."

"Wait until you have a baby coming, Jake." CJ pulled to a stop and turned off the engine. "Talk about a way to focus on the future."

"I look forward to having bambinos. Hey, guess what, you guys? Your kid will be approximately the same age as this raptor sanctuary."

"That'll make it easy to remember when the center was founded. Just don't expect Izzy and me to name this baby Hawk or Owl." He opened his door and started to climb down.

"Speak for yourself." Izzy opened her door, too. "Hawk would be a cool name for a boy."

"Yeah, but..." CJ caught himself before he mentioned Izzy's hunch about having a girl. "I suppose Hawk would be okay. Owl, not so much." He got out and hurried around to Izzy's side.

She was already down and had pulled back the seat to give Jake room to climb out.

Turning, Jake hauled out the cooler. "Are we sitting on the tailgate?"

"Guess so." CJ ushered Izzy around to the back of the truck and lowered the tailgate with a clang. "I forgot to bring chummy stumps."

"No worries." Hoisting the cooler into the truck bed, Jake swung up next to it and unlatched the lid. "It would be good to have a few out here for future use, though."

Izzy's eyebrows lifted. "What are chummy stumps?"

"Makeshift stools." Jake unfolded a red and white checked tablecloth. "When we need to take down a big pine, we saw the trunk into pieces we can use as outdoor stools. Henri asked us to do it and that's what she calls them."

"That's very cute. Very ranch-like, too." She gripped the side of the truck and started to put her foot on the bumper.

"Want a boost?"

Glancing over her shoulder, she gave him a smile, lowered her foot and turned toward him. "Sure."

Maybe she wanted him to touch her as much as he wanted to. That would be nice. Grasping her around the waist, he lifted her up and settled her on the tailgate.

"Thanks."

He held her gaze. "Anytime." *Anywhere. I'm yours for the taking.*

22

Anytime. Sounded like a promise. Whenever Isabel needed CJ, he'd be there for her. What woman wouldn't cherish such devotion?

Perched on the tailgate of a pickup between two gorgeous cowboys on a sunny day in June didn't suck, either. She hadn't solved any of her problems. On the contrary, she'd created a bigger one.

But at this very moment she was in a happy place, munching sandwiches Jake and CJ had made and discussing the raptors who would eventually benefit from the sanctuary.

Jake sat a respectful distance away from her, but CJ had moved in close, his thigh resting against hers and his shoulder and arm brushing hers when he moved. Cozy. Every so often he caught her gaze and smiled.

Evidently he was in a happy place, too. She wanted that for him, always. If only he could find that happy place with her in Seattle. She wanted it to be possible and yet she couldn't see it working. He belonged here.

During the discussion about raptors, she contributed what she'd learned from the countless hours she and Naomi had watched the eagle cam. Jake was the expert in the group, though. He'd been researching ever since January, when Zane had proposed creating an arm of Raptors Rise on the Buckskin.

"Thanks to Zane, I'm getting a crash course in birds of prey," Jake said. "I was never much of a student in school, but I'm devouring the books and videos he recommended."

She put down her sandwich and picked up her cider. "Looks like you found your calling."

"Another one, anyway. I still love ranch work and cooking, but these birds are fascinating." He gestured toward her empty plate. "How about another sandwich? We made plenty."

"Thanks, but I'll stop with two, which is twice as much as I used to eat. Great sandwiches, guys. Juicy tomatoes and sliced avocado just make it for me."

"CJ's a genius with a knife. Nobody slices a ripe heirloom or a buttery avocado like he does. Takes a deft touch to do it right."

She turned and gave him a once-over. "It's a valuable talent you have there, cowboy."

He winked. "Yes, ma'am."

Just like that, she was ready to haul him off into the bushes.

"Speaking of food," CJ cupped her knee in his large hand. "Jake's making chuck wagon stew tomorrow night at the bunkhouse. Since the weather's warmed up, we serve it outside by the fire pit. Want to join in?"

"Love to." The warmth of his hand on her knee traveled up her thigh and settled in a sensitive spot he'd visited several times the night before. "Can't pass up a chance to taste that famous stew. Will Lucy and Millie be there?"

"Yep. And Kate." CJ gave her knee a squeeze and moved his hand. "We'll ask Henri, too, but she may be partied out by then."

"Because of the shower?"

"No, it's the doings *after* the shower. This Thursday is the Babes' monthly sleepover. The shower fits nicely into their plans because they were already scheduled to be at Henri's."

"I've heard about this event. Lucy went to her first one last month. She said it was like a high-school slumber party on steroids." With the sleepover taking place later, the shower likely wouldn't run late. More time with CJ.

"Those ladies are a kick," Jake said. "Generous and kind, too. They gave Millie and me a set of dishes as a housewarming present. Once the cabin is in shape, we'll have them over for a meal."

"Isn't your cabin close to this site?"

"Walking distance."

"Then why can't I see it from here?"

"Look to your left, through the grove of aspens."

She peered in that direction. "Nothing but trees over there."

"Look closer. It has a forest green tin roof."

"Oh! There it is. I thought it would be like the guest cabins, built with horizontal logs. I've never seen one where the logs are vertical."

"The style is called palisade. Since the logs are upright, they look a little more like trees. And they're aspen so they really blend in."

"Neat idea. Henri said you guys were watching construction videos. Are you and Millie doing all the work yourselves?"

"We are."

CJ grinned. "Tell the lady how that's going, bro."

"It's going...well."

"Millie calls it a team-building exercise," CJ said. "It's been our entertainment for the past six weeks."

"Glad to oblige." Jake rolled his eyes.

"What's the story?"

"Sadly, Isabel, I'm a control freak. I want to do everything myself. I promised Millie the cabin would be a shared project. If I start taking over, she calls me on it." He sighed and gestured toward CJ. "And these guys back her up. They're relentless."

"That's...wow. Sounds like tough duty. And you say it's going well?

"Relatively speaking." He leaned forward to consult with CJ. "How many fights have Millie and I had about the cabin, bro? I'm losing count."

"I'd have to look at the scoreboard to be sure, but if you add the little spats and the major battles, maybe fifteen or sixteen."

Isabel gasped. "The Brotherhood keeps a *scoreboard*? That's funny and awful at the same time. Wouldn't it be easier to hire a contractor and reduce the stress on both of you?"

"Easier, sure, but building this cabin with Millie is making me a better man. By the time it's finished, I might be in good enough shape to marry that wonderful woman."

"But all that fighting...."

"And all that making up." Jake smiled. "That's the fun part. Now when we fight, I don't worry so much because we always make up."

"That's lovely, Jake." She touched his arm, impressed by his openness. "Thank you for sharing something so personal. Especially since you've only known me a short time."

"That's true on paper, but you come highly recommended by Lucy and you're having a baby with CJ. You're one of us, now." He met her gaze. "Whether you wanna be or not."

Her throat tightened. "I wanna be."

"Good." Breaking eye contact, he glanced at the angle of the sun. "I guess we'd better check out my pathway." He chuckled. "And it is mine, damn it. I have complete control."

She helped pack up the remains of the lunch and CJ put the cooler in the truck.

Reaching in his back pocket, Jake pulled out two crude maps and gave them each one. "It would help me more if you do this one at a time, so you don't influence each other's opinion." He glanced at CJ. "You first, bro. Check out the area, in case...well, just check it out."

Isabel picked up on the look that passed between the two men. "For snakes?"

CJ shrugged. "We have 'em. It'd be good for me to take a look-see. Do they make you nervous?"

"A little, but I'll bet I make them nervous, too. I won't run screaming if I see one. I'll just avoid it."

Respect gleamed in his eyes. "Want to go first, then?"

She laughed. "I can do without the adrenalin rush, thanks. I'm happy to let you go first."

"Glad to." He glanced at Jake. "What exactly do you want to know?"

"Whether the route makes sense to you," Jake said. "Do you like the order of the birds, do you think the amount of cover is adequate in the areas where I plan to put the enclosures, stuff like that."

Isabel stayed by the truck with Jake while CJ headed off, following Jake's map.

Ah, CJ. Everything about him turned her on—his loose-hipped stride, his wear-softened jeans that hugged his tight buns, his broad shoulders that stretched the plaid fabric of his shirt.

"He's nuts about you."

She looked over at Jake. "I really like him, too."

"Seems like it judging from your expression just now." He took a breath. "He's determined to be a full-time dad, and when CJ sets his mind on something...."

"He told me his mom let him do whatever he wanted."

"He's a lot better about accepting disappointment these days, especially with small things. But I don't see him accepting all those miles between him and his baby. Or the distance between you two, for that matter. He really cares for you."

"I know he does." Her muscles tensed. "But he wouldn't adapt to Seattle. He wants what you and Millie have, what Matt and Lucy have, a log cabin in the woods, preferably on Buckskin land."

"He also wants you and the baby." Jake's voice was kind but firm. "If you refuse to let him move there, you'll break his heart."

"If I let him move there, I'll kill his soul."

"I'm done!" CJ called out. "Not saying a word until you go along the path, Iz. It's all yours." He strode toward them, his color high, his gray eyes lit with excitement. "What a great project, Jake. I can't wait to see it in operation."

But would he? The visitor center was only a few stakes in the ground. The path and the enclosures were in the early planning stage. At best, the sanctuary wouldn't open until fall. If CJ got his way, he'd be in Seattle by then.

"Your turn, Iz." His smile was relaxed and carefree. The wide-open spaces of Montana had that effect on him. Who would he be in an urban setting? Would he still be CJ?

23

CJ gave Izzy a quick kiss at her door and promised to be in the cabin waiting for her when she came home from the baby shower. Then he loped back to the truck, climbed in and glanced at Jake, who'd moved up front. "Give it to me straight, bro."

"She's in love with you."

"*Yes.*" He slapped the steering wheel and gave Jake a big smile. "That's such good news." He started the engine and pulled away.

"Not necessarily."

"What do you mean? If she loves me, I'm in! She'll want me in her life, both as a father for our baby and as her loving husband. Which I will be, because I'm in—"

"Hold your horses, CJ. That's not always how love works. That's something I had to learn the hard way."

"Hey, I know you and Millie had a rough time, but your issues aren't my issues. Izzy and I will get along fine living together. I don't see big obstacles there."

"I don't either, if you ever get to that point. But your chances of a happily-ever-after are slim to none. She—"

"How can you say that? She's in love with me. That's all I need to know. Full steam a—"

"Listen for a minute, damn it. And slow down. You're kicking up a rooster tail."

"Okay." He eased off the gas pedal. "I'm listening."

"It's *because* she's in love with you that this relationship will go down in flames."

He pulled up to the barn and shut off the engine. "That makes no sense."

"She wants whatever is best for you and she's firmly convinced that what's best is working at the Buckskin and living in Apple Grove."

"I know. She's said that to me, too. If she's going to reject me out of love, I just have to overcome that argument with one of my own."

"Which is?"

"My love for her and our baby is stronger than my love for this place and the folks who live here." He gazed at Jake. "I don't mean that to be hurtful, but—"

"No need to explain, bro. That's the way it should be if you intend to spend your life with her. If I had to choose between the Brotherhood and Millie, I'd take Millie every time. Luckily I don't have to make that choice."

"And I don't, either. Not really. Living in Seattle won't change how I feel about everybody. It just changes my location."

"She doesn't see it that way. She views it as ripping you out by the roots and sticking you in a pot that's too small."

"She said that?"

"Not in so many words, but it's the impression she gave me."

"I could use that idea. What if I tell her I'm looking forward to transplanting my roots into her fertile soil? That's poetic, right?"

Jake snorted. "No, that's a bad pickup line. I wouldn't try to get fancy. Tell her you can't imagine life without her and the baby."

"It's true. I can't."

"Going out to the sanctuary site didn't help. You were way too enthusiastic about the project."

"But I *am* enthusiastic about it. What's wrong with that?"

"I'll wager she sees it as one more thing you'd be giving up. Same with chuck wagon stew night. Watching you goof around with us will help convince her that this is where you belong."

"Are you saying I should take her out for pizza instead? Because I—"

"Not an option. You've already set it up that you two are having dinner with the gang."

"The exact point I was about to make. I can't start acting like my life at the Buckskin doesn't matter anymore. She'd see right through that. I just need to show her that the Buckskin and Apple Grove are important, but she and the baby are more important."

"There you go. Forget roots and fertile soil. Just speak from your heart." Jake heaved a sigh and opened his door. "We'd better get cracking. Those stalls won't muck themselves."

"I predict they will someday." He climbed down and followed Jake into the barn. "They have self-cleaning litter boxes for cats."

"And you know this how?"

"My mom and I had a cat. Mom bought this motorized contraption that automatically scooped the box."

"Did it work?"

"Not with Caesar. He—"

"Of course she named him Caesar. Did you have a dog named Marc Anthony, too?"

"We did."

"You go, Cleopatra! I wish I'd known your mom, Cornelius, even if she did spoil you rotten. She must have been fun."

"She was."

"What happened with the self-cleaning litter box?"

"Caesar heard the motor and turned into the Tasmanian Devil. What a mess."

Jake nodded. "That's about what I'd expect. Picture a robotic stall mucker near a high-strung stallion like Thunderbolt. He'd reduce it to rubble. Nice idea but totally impractical."

"Wait and see. It'll happen."

"But not today. Grab a wheelbarrow, bro."

* * *

Two sweaty hours later, CJ and Jake each snagged a jug of water and headed outside for a ten-minute break. CJ leaned against the hitching post and gulped down at least a third of the gallon jug without pausing. Then he took off his hat and poured a little over his head, letting it dribble over his face and down his bare chest where his shirt hung open.

Jake did the same. Taking a bandana from his back pocket, he wiped his face. "Bet this is the hottest day so far this year."

"Let's check the temp." He pulled out his phone. Yikes, a text from Izzy, about an hour old. He'd missed the little pinging sound. Should have changed it to a trumpet blast.

"What's the temperature, bro?"

"Tell you after I read this text from Izzy and send a response."

Roaster stuck in traffic jam caused by a ten-car pileup. Highway patrol set up a detour. Winding roads. I'm nervous. Naomi's calm. How weird is that?

He quickly texted back. *Is it there yet?*

Not yet. Hope they anchored it well.

What could he say? *I'm sure they did.* He wasn't sure at all.

She sent him an emoji making a face.

Jake straightened and took another swig from his jug. "What's up with Isabel?"

"Her roaster's taking a detour instead of the highway. Winding roads. She's worried."

"I would be, too. Any glitch like that gets you to thinking the whole plan might fall apart."

"She said her sister's calm, though."

"Yeah, but her sister's ass isn't on the line."

"Maybe not financially, but getting this problem resolved is important to her."

"Well, sure. Hope it turns out okay, for everyone's sake."

"Me, too. Listen, I'm going over to Izzy's cabin to wait for her tonight. I'd like to make the place look romantic. I could ask Millie what she would suggest, but you're handy. How would you go about it?"

"Candles, for one thing. Millie greeted me with candles the first night we stayed together. And she had a fire going, but you don't want to light a fire tonight."

CJ laughed. "Yes, I do."

"In the fireplace, smartass. Do you have time to go into town?"

"Yeah. I'm off at five."

"Then pick up some apple-scented votives at the Apple Barrel. Buy a bunch, a dozen if they have that many. More is better with candles. Maybe look for a bottle of fake champagne at the market."

"Non-alcoholic?"

"Yeah, that. Borrow an ice bucket, a stand and a couple of flutes from Kate. Make it look classy even if it is the fake kind."

"Okay. Keep going."

"Cue up a romantic playlist on your phone and...hold on, what am I saying? You play guitar, bro. You could serenade her."

"That might look great in the movies, but I can't imagine pulling it off. Maybe if I made my living that way I'd have the cojones to perform for her. I damn near asked to join the band on Tuesday night. Glad I didn't."

"Then forget that. I see your point. Go with the playlist on your phone, then. You could ask her to dance."

"I like that idea."

"Some guys scatter rose petals around. I'm not into roses, but you could see if they have any for sale at the market."

"Have you noticed those don't have much smell to 'em?"

"No, because I don't do roses."

"Henri's roses smell way better. I'd rather ask her if I can have two or three off her bushes, and maybe gather up any petals that have fallen on the ground so I have some to scatter."

"Better handle that before the shower starts." He grinned. "You don't want to be spotted lurking around Henri's bushes and crawling around on the ground picking up rose petals. That's not manly."

"I'll get that part done early. Assuming I end up with a bunch of rose petals, where do I scatter them?"

"I guess you throw 'em anywhere and everywhere. Fling 'em in the air like confetti for all I know."

"Now *that's* not manly."

"Whatever. The rose petal distribution is up to you."

"Is that it, then?"

"Chocolate's a nice touch, but she'll be sugared up from the treats at the baby shower. I'd skip the chocolate."

"Good call."

"Pulling out all the stops, are you?"

"You know what I'm up against. Wouldn't you?"

"I suppose I would." He gazed at him. "I feel for you, bro. Thank God I'm way past the torture you're going through."

"Worth it, though, right?"

"Absolutely worth it. But at the time I had my doubts."

"I've got you beat, then. I have no doubts. And I'll do whatever it takes."

24

"Okay, sis. The worst is over."

"I won't relax until Fred gets it running." Isabel glanced at the time. Ten to six. Lucy would show up at six to escort her over to Henri's.

"Fred will be here any minute," Naomi said. "While the guys put the door back on, I'll walk around your new roaster so you can see for yourself it arrived in perfect shape."

"That would be great." She focused on the screen. "Move back a little. Good. Terrific view. It really does look new. Now it just has to work."

"It will." The voice was familiar.

"Bob Kennedy? Is that you?"

"It's him." Naomi swung the phone toward Bob, who gave her a wave. He looked to be in his sixties, fit and attractive. Naomi turned the phone around and her face filled the screen. "Bob's a sweetheart. He followed the truck down to make sure everything went like clockwork."

"Which it *didn't*, of course," Bob said, although he sounded cheerful about it.

"Bob's smiling." Naomi turned the phone in his direction. "He's been good for morale."

"Your sister is, too, Isabel," Bob said. "Great business you have here. Since I attempted this and gave it up as too much work, I can imagine the hours you've spent creating such a successful venue."

"Thank you. I have put in a lot of blood, sweat and tears. Naomi, too. I couldn't have done it without her."

"Thanks, Izzy. That's sweet. Hey, Fred's here!" She moved the phone again. "Say hi to Izzy, Fred."

"Hey, Isabel." His craggy face appeared on the screen. "Don't worry about a thing. Because the roaster's been in service, it won't need to be seasoned. You can put it straight into production, like you did with the previous one. Saves time."

Isabel blinked. "That's true. I can't believe I didn't remember that."

"I did." Naomi sounded a little smug, which was her right.

"Naomi, you're a genius. Now if Fred can get things rolling..."

Naomi's face appeared in the screen. "He's on it. But Lucy's due any minute, right?"

"She just tapped on the door. She's a little early. I'll ask her if we can wait until the roaster's operational before we leave. Hang on a sec." She went to the door and opened it.

Lucy was decked out like a rhinestone cowgirl, sparkles on her shirt and on her jeans. She pointed to the phone Isabel held in her hand. "Naomi?"

"Yeah." Isabel stood back and beckoned her in. "Our maintenance guy is hooking up the new roaster. Could you please text Henri and tell her we'll be there as soon as the roaster is working? Shouldn't be long."

"Glad to." She stepped inside and pulled out her phone.

"Tell Lucy hi for me," Naomi said.

"You can tell her hi, yourself." Isabel waiting until Lucy finished with her text before handing over her phone. "Naomi wants to say hello."

"Sure thing. Hey, Naomi! I hear you're working miracles in that coffee shop."

While Lucy chatted with Naomi, Isabel took several deep breaths and rolled her tight shoulders. If the next few minutes went well, the crisis would be over.

Lucy chuckled. "Yeah, I'll bet. But you pulled it out of the fire, girlfriend."

Lucy clearly admired Naomi's response in a difficult situation. Rightly so. She'd tackled the issue head-on, listened to valuable advice from Fred, a trusted colleague, and taken decisive action. Maybe it was time to ask her if she wanted in as a full partner.

"I'll turn you back over to Izzy," Lucy said. "Take care, Naomi, and congratulations." Lucy held out the phone. "You might want to charge this soon."

Isabel glanced at the battery indicator. "God, you're right. This is twice now I've let it run way down. I never do that." She focused on Naomi. "How's Fred doing?"

"He's almost got it."

"Has the shop been busy this afternoon?"

"It was until recently, but it's slow now, thank goodness. The tech conference folks have some big-deal dinner tonight. They'll be back around nine, but this drama will be over by then, so we...wait...woo-hoo! Iz, the roaster works like a charm!"

"Thank the Lord." Isabel let out a breath. "Give Fred *another* hug for me."

"I will!" Naomi turned off the video. "We're having a hug fest with everybody, Izzy— Fred, Bob, George, me. In a few minutes, I'll invite the rest of the staff back here. They've been on pins and needles."

"Haven't we all. Maybe we should throw a staff party when I get back. And Fred's invited."

"How about me?" Bob called out.

"You, too, Bob."

"We're all up for a party," Naomi said. "Can't wait to see you again, sis."

"Same here, Naomi. I'm so grateful for you."

"I wasn't about to let the shop go to hell while you were gone."

"Obviously! Have yourself a nice, relaxing evening."

"You, two, Iz. Are you seeing CJ tonight?"

"Yes. After the shower."

"I'm glad. 'Bye, sis. Love you."

"Love you, too. See you soon." She disconnected the call and went in search of her charger. Where was it? Ah. Kitchen counter.

Should she take her phone and the charger to Henri's? No. Naomi had the situation in hand. Even if some issue cropped up, she'd handle it. What a relief.

She glanced at Lucy and smiled. "Let's party!"

* * *

Picking the roses and gathering petals had taken CJ longer than he'd anticipated, but he finished before anyone arrived for the baby shower. Henri had loaned him a water-filled vase for the roses and a bowl for the petals. He drove back to the bunkhouse with the vase wedged between his thighs so it wouldn't dump.

Leo and Garrett were fixing what smelled like fried chicken. CJ's stomach rumbled. "Smells great." He walked into the kitchen carrying the vase and bowl.

Garrett had two skillets going. He glanced over his shoulder. "Aw, you shouldn't have."

"He *really* shouldn't have," Leo said. "Those are Henri's roses. I hope you asked her first, bro."

"I asked and she even loaned me a vase, but they're not for you guys. I want to leave them in the fridge while I pick up some other things in town."

"Dinner's in fifteen minutes," Garrett said. "Might as well stay for some chicken and potato salad."

"Can't. Need to get to the market before it closes." He set the vase and bowl on the counter while he made room for them in the fridge.

"Maybe we have whatever it is you're going after," Leo said. "You could replace it later."

"I'd bet my next paycheck we don't have any fake champagne."

"Ah." Garrett smiled. "Now the rose petals make more sense. You're planning a welcome home for Isabel."

"That's the plan." Tucking the vase next to the hard cider and the bowl behind a large one filled with potato salad, he started to close the door and paused. "Can I have some potato salad?"

"By all means," Leo said. "You need to keep up your strength."

CJ shot him a look before grabbing a bowl from the cupboard and spoon from the silverware drawer. He scooped out a generous portion, replaced the serving bowl and shut the fridge door. "The thing is, I've never set up a romantic scene before." He dug into his potato salad.

"You've got a good start," Garrett said. "Pretty roses and extra petals to scatter around."

"But where do I scatter them? Jake suggested getting some but he was clueless about the deployment." He shoved another spoonful into his mouth.

Leo shrugged. "Don't look at me. I've never set up a romantic scene, either. That's what happens, or rather what doesn't happen, when you live in a bunkhouse."

"Depends on how many rose petals you have." Garrett picked up tongs and started turning the chicken. "I didn't get a good look at that bowl."

CJ chewed and swallowed. "I didn't count, but I'd estimate I have about twenty-five or thirty petals."

"Then you don't want to waste them making a trail from the door to the bed. That's an option, but only if you have two or three times that many."

"Had to cut the gathering detail short so early arrivals wouldn't see my ass sticking out of the bushes."

Leo ducked his head.

"Go ahead and laugh, bro. I was laughing at myself, down on all fours pawing through dead leaves to find viable petals. Especially when I don't know what the hell to do with them."

Garrett flipped the last few pieces of chicken and turned away from the stove. "Fold back the top sheet and sprinkle them over the bottom sheet."

"Really?"

"Sure. They'll smell nice and the red will look pretty against the white sheets."

"Shouldn't I wash them, first?"

Leo's shoulders began to shake and he let out a snort.

"I know that sounds ridiculous, but these came off the ground and I'm pretty sure Henri uses manure on those roses."

"That's a valid point I hadn't considered." Garrett looked like he was ready to lose it, too. He cleared his throat. "Finish your potato salad and take off. We'll wash the rose petals and have them waiting for you."

"You'll really wash them, right? You won't just say you did."

"We'll really wash them. We'll—"

"Wait!" Leo's eyes widened. "You can't wash them in the *sink,* dude. He's right about the manure."

"Then we'll wash them in the shower."

"How?"

"I'll figure it out."

"I say CJ should forget the petals, or pluck some off the ones in the vase."

"No way am I plucking those roses baldheaded. Not after I stuck myself about twenty times cutting them and putting them in the vase. Gonna hurt like hell next time I play my guitar."

"No worries, CJ," Garrett said. "Leo and I will wash the ones in the bowl."

"Better wash the bowl good, too," Leo muttered, "or you'll have cross-contamination."

CJ sighed. "This rose petal thing better be worth it."

"It is." Garrett turned back to the stove.

"Why?" He went to the sink and rinsed his bowl.

Garrett glanced at him. "You'll find out."

"If you say so. Thanks for washing the petals. I'll be back in less than an hour."

"We could save you a couple pieces of chicken," Leo said.

"Thanks, but the potato salad will do. I'll need to shower and shave before I head over there and I want to leave myself plenty of time to set up before she gets back."

"You didn't ask someone to text you when she's leaving the party?"

"No, and by now everyone's there so I don't want to text anybody now."

"Kate's not there yet. She can't leave until the guest dining room's shipshape."

"Good thinking, Leo." CJ pulled out his phone and sent the request. Kate texted him a thumbs-up. "Thanks, guys. I didn't think this would turn out to be so complicated."

"That's love for you," Garrett said.

"Yep." No point in denying he was in up to his eyeballs. "But tonight's designed to simplify things." He hurried out to his truck and headed for town.

25

"Third time's a charm." Isabel held a mixing bowl full of dried rice in her lap. Signaling Lucy to start the timer, she closed her eyes and plunged her hand into the rice. "I have you, my pretty!" She slid a safety pin to the rim of the bowl. Except it wasn't a pin. Just a few grains of rice. "Auugghh!"

Josette threw her hands in the air. "*C'est diabolique!*"

"You said it." Isabel handed the bowl to Ed, the last contestant. "Can't believe I couldn't locate one out of...how many?"

"I put in twenty," Pam said. "But now there's only nineteen since I...."

"Yeah, yeah." Peggy stretched her long legs in front of her and took a sip from her hard cider. "Admit it. You practiced all afternoon."

"I can't help it if I'm blessed with a sophisticated sense of touch." Pam had pinned it to the collar of her Western shirt like a badge. It winked in the light from paper lanterns strung overhead in Henri's backyard.

"I'm sure as hell practicing before we play this again," Red grumbled. "And we *are* playing it again next week so I can redeem myself."

"I vote for that," Henri said. "We'll save the rice and pins in a Ziploc and schedule a rematch next week."

"I volunteer to keep the Ziploc," Millie toyed casually with a lock of her red hair, her expression innocent.

"Nice try, girlfriend." Kate grinned. "You don't get the rice and pins."

"Technically they're my rice and pins," Pam said. "So I should—"

"Sorry." Peggy shook her head. "This rice and pin combo is hereby declared the official property of the Babes. It goes in Henri's safe."

"Ah," Josette said, "but can *Henri* be trusted?"

"I can, but I couldn't cram one more thing in that safe. Unless you want to tuck the bag of rice inside our autographed Tim McGraw Stetson."

A chorus of *noooo* ended that discussion.

"We'll let the Brotherhood keep it." Pam walked over to a washtub full of drinks and pulled out a bottle of cider. "Isabel, can I offer you a virgin one of these?"

"Sure, thanks."

After twisting off the top, Pam brought it over. "I'm sorry you didn't find a pin. It's harder than it looks. I—"

"Got it!" Ed held up a safety pin. "On the second try! Which means I get one more chance." She pinned the trophy on her collar and signaled Lucy. "Go." She shoved her hand in the rice.

All conversation stopped. The only sounds were the chirp of crickets and the rustle of Ed sifting the rice.

"Bingo!" Ed held up a second pin. Grinning in triumph, she stuck it on the other side of her collar. "Now I'm balanced."

Pam stared at her in open-mouthed shock. "You said you'd never played this!"

"That's a fact. I like it, though. Fun game."

"Only you, Ed." Peggy gave her a bemused smile. "Is there anything you're *not* good at?"

"Tons of things. Evidently this isn't one of them."

"I've played this a bunch of times," Pam said. "I've never seen a first-timer snag two pins."

Ed settled back in her lawn chair. "Well, now you have. What do I get?"

"Oh!" Henri left her chair. "I forgot I picked up something for prizes. Be right back."

Ed leaned over toward Isabel. "I love getting prizes."

"I understand you've won quite a few."

"Last month she got another trophy," Josette said. "Took first place in a barrel racing competition in Billings."

"Your third place is nothing to sneeze at, Josie." Ed gave her a thumbs-up. "And the rest of you were *this close* to placing." She measured a fraction of an inch with her fingers. "Next time you'll—"

"Ta-da! Here comes your prize!" Henri sashayed out of the house with a plush moose about eight inches tall balanced on a fancy silver tray.

"Awesome!" Ed clapped her hands together. "I've been meaning to buy one of those ever since Ben got them in at the Moose!"

"Now you don't have to." Henri held out the tray. "Your Choosy Moose, madam."

"Thank you." Ed picked up the moose. "Is this a male or a female?"

"Does it matter?"

"Of course it matters. I need to choose a name."

"Let me see it." Red came over, took the moose and turned it bottoms up. "You'd better go gender neutral."

"Okay. Then Merle Moose it is."

"Great idea, Henri," Peggy said. "I forgot we'd need prizes. We can all settle up with you later."

"No settling necessary. When Ben found out what this was for, he donated several to the cause."

"Because he's sweet on you." Ed tucked the moose next to her hip. "You need to put the poor man out of his misery."

Henri laughed. "You want me to shoot him?"

"I want you to date him. I hate to see such a lovely man suffer that way."

"We've known each other too long. Dating him would be weird." Henri glanced around. "Who's ready for the next game?"

"Me," Isabel said. "I want a moose."

* * *

An hour later, after hugging everyone and thanking them about a thousand times, Isabel climbed in the passenger seat of Millie's sedan with a bag of shower gifts and a plush moose. Since Lucy was staying for the sleepover, Millie had offered to drop Isabel off on her way home.

"I had such a great time, Millie." Isabel sighed and leaned back against the seat. "I can't imagine a more fun baby shower."

"Thank goodness the weather held and we could put up the lanterns. I plan to string lanterns on the porch of our cabin as soon as we're done applying the finish."

"I saw your place through the trees today, but Jake had to point it out. He told me what the perpendicular log style is called, but I've already forgotten it."

"Palisade. That was one thing we agreed on right away. Other things, we've had to hammer out."

"I heard about the scoreboard."

"Yeah? Did he mention it or CJ?"

"CJ's the one who used the word, but only after Jake asked for a tally of your arguments."

"He didn't mind discussing it?"

"Didn't seem to, although I was surprised that he was so open with me. I was touched, too."

"It's very cool that he was willing to talk about it, especially with someone who's not...." She paused. "I mean, someone who hasn't—"

"It's okay, Millie. Everyone's been terrific, but clearly I don't have the long history that the rest of you have. Well, Garrett only arrived two months ago, but everyone else has years of shared experiences to draw on. Jake was kind enough to say I was one of you since CJ and I are having a baby, but—"

"Isabel, you are one of us. We all liked you so much when you came for Lucy and Matt's wedding. Even though you didn't plan on this baby, it's an exciting turn of events."

"Thanks for saying that." She heaved a sigh. "I'm excited, too. I only wish it hadn't put CJ in a difficult position."

"He seems to be rolling with it."

Rolling in the wrong direction. She didn't say it, though. No reason to bring up—

"Just so you know, I see your side of it."

"You do?" Startled, she looked over at Millie. "I thought everybody—"

"I see his side, too. But putting myself in your shoes, I wouldn't want to live with a man who's sacrificed his happiness for me, especially if I'm in love with him."

She gulped. "Is it that obvious?"

"It was to Jake this afternoon."

Her heartbeat quickened. "Evidently he told you, but did he tell—"

"Yes."

"Oh." She took a shaky breath. "That'll make CJ even more determined to move."

"Probably."

"His iron will is part of the problem. I can see him getting to Seattle and forcing himself to stay even if he's miserable."

"He's capable of that, but what if it goes the other way? What if the joy of being with his new little family overrides the negatives and he's blissfully happy?"

"That's so unlikely."

"But it's not impossible. By the way, we're here."

"I knew that." She gave Millie a sheepish smile. "I need to let you get home to Jake. I just—"

"You'd like a chance to gather your forces before going in to face him?"

"Yeah."

"Take your time."

"Until now, I didn't fully appreciate how interconnected all of you are."

"Oh, yeah. Especially the Brotherhood."

"That's my point! CJ would be leaving those guys, leaving Henri, you and Kate, the Babes, his entire support system."

"In body, but not in spirit. Henri loves that her boys are sticking around, but she says they're fully capable of building a life elsewhere. Seth has proven that. She says if they aren't, then she and Charley failed."

"I'll take that into consideration, too." Isabel reached for the door handle. "Since you have so much inside information...is CJ going to pull out a ring tonight?"

"Not that I know of."

She let out a breath. "I sure hope he doesn't." She opened the door and got out, hauling her bag with her. "Thanks for the ride and the empathy."

"Anytime."

"See you tomorrow." Closing the door, she gave Millie a wave and started toward the porch steps. He'd dimmed the lights. Only a subtle glow penetrated the drawn curtains. She gulped and kept walking.

As Millie pulled away, CJ opened the door. Country music drifted out, a slow love song. "Looks like you have loot."

Clearly he'd set the scene for... something. Her heart thundered in her ears. "They gave me so many nice gifts. Luckily baby stuff is small so I should be able to get everything in my suitcase." She climbed the steps.

Crossing the porch, he reached for the bag. "Let me take that."

She caught a whiff of his aftershave. Judging from his bristle-free chin, he'd shaved and likely showered, too. She breathed in the heady scent as she handed over the bag.

His gaze traveled over her and he smiled. "Water fight?"

"Bobbing for apples." She glanced down at the forgotten water spots on her orange shirt. "I won." Looking up, she tucked her wet hair behind her ears. "Got a little plush moose as a prize."

He grinned. "Congratulations. Sounds like you had a good time."

"I really did." She glanced past him to the light flickering from the interior of the cabin. "Did you build a fire?"

"Too hot for that. Come on in." He drew her through the open door and nudged it closed with his foot.

She gasped. "CJ!"

"Do you like it?"

"The room looks beautiful." *Please don't let this be the prelude to a proposal.* "You've been busy."

"Kind of."

"Great job." A vase of fragrant roses sat on the nightstand along with his phone, the source of the romantic music. The aroma of the roses mingled with another sweet smell, maybe from the candles.

No wonder he'd turned off the lights. Didn't need them with all those candles. Rose petals decorated the snowy white sheets and a bucket of champagne rested on a stand beside the bed.

She turned to him. "You're making me nervous."

"Nervous? Why?"

"I'm afraid any minute you'll drop to one knee and pull a velvet box out of your pocket."

His eyes widened. "You think I'm about to propose?"

"That's what this looks like!" She swept an arm around the room. "Candles, roses, champagne, mood music...what else am I supposed to think?"

"Not that! We're a *long* way from that step."

Air whooshed out in a sigh of relief. "Thank goodness."

"But not so far from this one." He reached for her and pulled her close. His warm gaze held hers captive. "I love you, Isabel Marie Riccetti."

26

The glow of happiness in Izzy's eyes was encouraging. She hadn't popped right back with *I love you, too,* but he could wait for that. If Jake said she loved him, that was good enough for now.

She cupped his face in both hands. "I'm impressed that you went to all this trouble. Most guys—"

"I'm not most guys."

She brushed his cheeks with her thumbs. "That's for sure."

"I wanted the right setting. It's important. I've only said those words to my mother and Henri."

Her eyes widened. "Really?"

"I've been in lust with several, but it was never love on my part. If they felt more, they didn't say so."

Her gaze searched his. "Is it because of our baby?"

"Izzy, I was in love with you by the end of our first night together."

"How could you know? We had plenty of lust going on. What if it was an extreme case of—"

"Nope. The lust was a bonus on top of a much bigger feeling. Didn't know what it was, at first. Finally figured out what was different about you, about us."

"And?"

He tugged her closer. "In a crowd, we communicated with only a look or a smile. When we were alone, your eyes told me everything I needed to know. The way you responded to me...it was like you read my mind."

She nodded. "And like you read mine."

"I thought we would be the same when you headed down here again. Then you said we shouldn't have sex anymore. But your eyes said—"

"Something different." She gazed up at him. "I've never been a waffler. But now—"

"At least you didn't stick to the program." He rubbed the small of her back. "And sometimes I imagine I can still read your mind."

"I guess Jake can."

"Oh?"

"Millie gave me a ride home. She was very informative." Izzy didn't seem upset. Instead she was melting into him like warm wax. "Was that why you invited me to go out to the sanctuary site?"

"Not *the* reason, but one of them." He might as well spit out the truth. "I wanted to know where I stood. I honestly couldn't tell anymore. Jake agreed to gather intel. He drew a conclusion. Doesn't mean he's right, but I—"

"Doesn't mean he's wrong."

His breath caught. "Iz?"

"I've loved you since that first night, too."

Enough energy surged through him to power the Buckskin's generator for a month. "God, that's all I needed to hear. Now we can—"

"It doesn't change anything."

"Are you kidding? It changes *everything*. If we love each other, the sky's the limit! We—"

"If we love each other, we'll make good decisions about the future, because that's what people who love each other do."

"Why do I find that statement so depressing? Oh, I know. Because next you'll tell me the best decision is long-distance parenting."

"Because it *is*."

"I won't do it, Izzy." Despite their difference of opinion, he kept his grip firm. She'd have to demand that he release her before he'd let go. Sparring with her at close range was a better strategy. He had some really good songs coming up on his playlist. Her favorite.

"Well, I won't agree to you moving to Seattle."

"You need to think of Cleo." He began moving in time to the music.

"Who's Cleo?"

"Our daughter. Just throwing the name up as a trial balloon. I've been thinking about names and—"

"We don't know we'll have a girl."

"You know and that's enough for me." He moved her in a lazy circle around the small area between the front door and the bed. When she didn't resist, he took heart.

"Cleo. Short for Cleopatra."

"Yes, ma'am. I wouldn't want to saddle her with all of it. Cleo's nice. Goes with Marie, too. But you may not—"

"You know, I do like it. Cleo Marie. Are we dancing?"

"Seems like we are. We're moving and there's music, so we must be."

"You're a sneaky one, Cornelius Jasper, playing *She's My Kind of Rain*. You're trying to soften me up."

"Don't need to." He leaned down and nuzzled the side of her neck. "You're already soft enough."

Her breath hitched. "For what?"

"Rolling around on that bed, finding out how it feels when we crush rose petals under our writhing bodies."

"You've never tried it?'

"Have you?" If she'd done the rose petal thing with some other guy, he'd scoop them out of that bed and ditch the idea.

"I haven't, but I figured you had, since you set it up."

"I've never done it. I've been told it's worth the effort of collecting the petals."

"You did that?"

"I collected them. Garrett and Nick washed and dried them."

"Oh. My. God." Her eyes sparkled with laughter. "Those are Henri's roses, aren't they?"

"And her vase."

"The candles?"

"Jake's idea."

"The bucket of champagne?"

"Jake, again. Kate provided the bucket and stand. I've never created a setup like this so I needed a little help from my friends."

"Oh, CJ." She stopped dancing and stood on tiptoe to give him a tender kiss. "We're going to make love in a bed of roses."

"Yes, ma'am."

"What are we waiting for?" Wiggling out of his arms, she began pulling off her clothes.

He did the same. He'd learned that when Izzy took charge of the proceedings, he was wise to follow her lead.

She was naked before he was and that slowed him down considerably because he couldn't stop looking at her. What's more, she wanted him to.

"Watch this." Standing beside the bed in all her glory, arms out, she flopped backward onto the bed. She bounced and so did the red petals. "Ooo. I like this." Scooping up a few, she dribbled them over her breasts and stomach. "Hurry up, cowboy. Let's play."

He ditched the rest of his clothes in record time, letting them fall wherever. Holding her gaze, he approached the bed. "Have a game in mind?"

"I do. It's called *Driving CJ Crazy.*" She scooted over and patted the sheet, making the petals dance. "Lie on your back right here."

"Okay." He started to clear a spot so he could sit.

"No, leave them." She put back what he'd brushed aside. "See how it feels."

He eased down on the scattered petals and began to laugh. "Tickles."

"Lie down."

"Yes, ma'am." Grinning, he stretched out on his back. "They're still kinda wet."

"Wet and soft." Rolling to her side, she held her closed fist over his chest. Opening it gradually, she dribbled petals over his chest.

The sensation itself was erotic, but he was even more turned on by her expression. Her gaze hot and her lips parted, she went back for more petals and decorated his abs, his crotch and his thighs.

Her breathing quickened. "That's the sexiest visual *ever.*"

He reached for her. "How about if I—"

"Stay there. I'm coming over." She straddled his thighs and hummed with pleasure as she settled her tush on the petals she'd scattered there.

Talk about a sexy visual. Her breasts trembled with the rapid pace of her breathing. His breathing wasn't all that steady, either. If only she'd rise to her knees and edge a little bit forward, she could—

Instead she picked up more rose petals and let them cascade over his very erect cock.

He groaned.

"How does that feel?"

"Like butterfly wings."

"Is that good?"

"It's torture. I need—" He gasped as she dipped her head and bestowed an open-mouthed kiss on his bad boy.

"That?"

He clenched his jaw. "It's a start."

"How's this?" She took a petal and stroked lightly and thoroughly—the tip, the underside, and his aching balls.

"Izzy."

"The object of the game is to—"

"Mission accomplished."

"Good, because I'm driving myself crazy. I want you so bad, you rose-petal-covered man." Rising to her knees, she positioned herself and grabbed hold before taking him up to the hilt.

He battled the urge to come. Won the first round. "Iz…" The effort roughened his voice. "Hold still a minute."

"A minute?"

"Five seconds."

She counted them off, the little devil. Then she braced her hands on his chest and leaned down to lick his pecs and bite his nipples.

He spoke through gritted teeth. "You're gonna make me come."

"I don't care." Her voice was breathy, fanning his damp chest and moving the petals around. "I could come any second just looking at you."

"Why?"

"That ripped body is reason enough. Then add in rose petals resting lightly on your massive chest…okay, that's it. We're going for it."

"*Thank* you." Hallelujah, she'd stopped kidding around. Grasping her hips, he held on for dear life, fighting to outlast her. He lost that fight.

With a groan of surrender, he arched into her. "I...love...you!"

With a cry of triumph, she came, gasping as she leaned over him, her gaze locked with his. "I love you, too."

There it was, the perfect exchange while making perfect love. They were going to be just fine.

27

Isabel had fully intended to stay awake long enough to make love to CJ again. Maybe they'd drink some of that champagne and she'd show him the cool gifts she'd received.

But sometime during the after-sex cuddling, a routine CJ loved as much as she did, she fell asleep. When he woke her with a kiss, he was dressed.

Confused, she propped herself on her elbow. "Is it morning?"

"'Fraid so. I have to go, but I promised not to leave without saying goodbye."

"Did we go to sleep with the candles burning?"

"No. When you drifted off I blew them out and turned off my phone."

"And didn't set an alarm?"

"I did, but I was awake before it went off."

She touched his bristly cheek. "You didn't wake me."

"I couldn't bear to. You looked so peaceful. Besides, you and the baby probably need the sleep."

"You're a good man, CJ."

"Who loves you very much."

"I can tell. And I love you, too, but—"

"Gotta go." He kissed her once more and started for the door.

"We didn't drink the champagne."

"We can take it over to the bunkhouse so you have something fun to drink with chuck wagon stew."

"Will I see you before then?"

He opened the door and paused. "I'll check the schedule and text you. I was so focused on last night's plans that I can't remember what I'm scheduled for today."

"Just let me know."

"I will. Grab some more sleep." He put on his hat, touched two fingers to the brim and ducked out the door.

Sleep? Not likely. She climbed out of bed and hurried over to the window to peek out through a slight gap in the curtain. Off he went, his stride purposeful. Then he lifted both arms and punched his fists into the air.

The image stayed with her as she showered. Her text from CJ showed up while she was toweling off.

Nick and I are taking a group out for a lunch ride today. No lunch break, but I'm off at four. Want to hang out at the bunkhouse and help Jake and me make the stew?

Absolutely! She added a kiss-blowing emoji.

He called. "I was hoping you were still in bed."

"Wasn't sleepy."

"Maybe because you're such a deep sleeper. You barely moved."

She laughed. "Did you keep track?"

"Kind of. I was too happy to sleep much. I kept waking up so I could look at you lying beside me."

A heart-melting confession. "That's very sweet." She cleared the tightness from her throat. "Will you be okay out on the trail?"

"Sure. I'll have Nick tie my wrists to the horn so I don't fall off."

"CJ!"

He laughed. "I'll be fine. Cowboys don't need a lot of sleep. Listen, gotta go. I'll come fetch you after work. Love you." He disconnected before she could respond.

But a response had been halfway to her lips. *Love you, too.* How easy to say it now that the dam had been breached. Not so easy to face the consequences, though.

She was still staring at her phone when it lit up with a message from Lucy.

Not sketching this morning. Want to go for short ride and then have breakfast at my cabin?

Yes. I can be ready in ten minutes. I'll bring my decaf coffee beans.

Perfect! Be there in ten.

Isabel dressed quickly in jeans, a T-shirt and her new boots. Giving her hair a quick blow-dry, she straightened up the cabin. She tucked the votives in an empty dresser drawer, put the champagne in the kitchen and dumped the water out of the bucket.

Last of all she scooped up all the rose petals she could find and dumped them in the trash. She'd never look at rose petals the same way again.

The rumble of a truck's engine announced Lucy's arrival. Isabel grabbed her hat and her bag of coffee beans before walking out on the porch. The deep blue paint job glittered in the light from the rising sun.

"Your truck's looking good, Luce." She put on her hat as she descended the porch steps.

"Better than I do, I'll bet." Lucy got out wearing shades in addition to a hat. "The Babes sure can party."

"How late did you guys stay up?"

"I crashed at two, but Henri said the rest of them didn't pack it in until past three. I'm clearly the weak link."

"Are they sleeping it off at Henri's?"

"Oh, no. They brewed some of your coffee, which they adore, by the way, and they were out of there early, ready to tackle their daily routine."

"That's impressive."

"I don't know how they do it. I have zero energy for sketching this morning. A nice gentle ride is all I'm up for. Thanks for keeping me company."

"Glad to. I wondered if I'd have another chance to ride before I leave."

"Can't believe it's Friday already. The week went fast." She gestured toward the truck. "Climb in."

Isabel grinned as she swung up into the passenger seat and closed the door. "I can see why you like driving this rig. The world looks different from here."

"Doesn't it?" Lucy put the truck in gear, backed out and headed down the road CJ had taken earlier. "When I first moved here and needed something to drive, I thought *Matt has a truck. I'll get a cute little car.* Then I saw Celeste on the lot, took her for a test drive, and decided Matt and I would be a two-truck family."

"It suits you. You've always been a take-charge woman and this is a take-charge vehicle."

"And she's beautiful, inside and out."

Isabel laughed. "Yes, she is."

"I have an ulterior motive for inviting you to go riding this morning."

"Good, because I have an ulterior motive for accepting the invitation."

"Because you need to talk about last night?"

"Desperately."

"Thank God. I didn't want to pry, but—"

"He didn't propose."

"He didn't? Ha! I bet right on that one."

"You mean literally bet?"

"Literally. I had five bucks that said he wouldn't propose. CJ would want to do it right with a ring and there's no way he could come up with a ring that fast."

"Who was betting?"

"Everybody—the Babes, Millie, Kate, the Brotherhood."

Isabel laughed. "I should have seen that coming, but I'm still the new girl in town. I haven't fully absorbed the culture."

"If he didn't propose, what was the deal with the candles, flowers and champagne?"

"He wanted the setting to be special when he said he loved me."

"Awww! All that for a declaration of love?"

"Yeah." Her throat tightened up again. "He's only said it to his mom and Henri. Announcing it to me was a big deal."

"And what did you say?"

"I admitted that I'm in love with him, too. He pretty much knew it, anyway. Jake told him I was."

"Any of us could have told him that, but having you confirm it must have made him happy."

"It did, until I said people who love each other make careful decisions about the future because they want the best for their loved one."

"Meaning you think his plan sucks for him."

"Yes, but I didn't put that fine a point on it."

"Did you guys argue?"

"No. We...danced. And made love."

"Huh." Lucy parked in front of the barn, shut off the motor and gave Isabel a long look. "Sounds like you might be reconsidering your position."

"I don't know. Maybe." She unlatched her seatbelt and turned. "Last night he couldn't sleep because he was so happy that I love him back. He told me he kept looking at me lying there asleep beside him."

"Wow, he *is* in love."

"Yeah, and when he left this morning, I went to the window so I could watch him walk away. As he headed down the road, he punched his fists in the air like Rocky."

"That's cute. And so are you, hurrying over to the window for one last glimpse."

"I'm a dork."

"A dork in love."

"It's true. CJ is just...so great. The thing is, he's happy now, but—"

"FYI, your happy guy is headed this way."

"He is?" She glanced out the passenger window and her breath caught. CJ sauntered toward the truck, his hat nudged back and his gaze trained on her. Then he smiled, filling her with warmth and sunshine. "I'm crazy about him, Luce."

"Looks like he's in the same condition. He might relocate whether you agree or not."

"Oh, he wouldn't do that."

"Are you sure?"

Before she could respond, CJ opened her door. "Hi, there." He offered his hand.

"Hi, yourself." His firm grip as he helped her down sent hot signals to her lady parts. "Thanks."

"My pleasure. Listen, I'll pick you up at four-thirty, if that's okay."

"Sure. Whenever you're ready. Are you going to play your guitar tonight? Lucy said you usually do."

"Would you like that?"

"I'd love it."

"Then I will."

"Hey, CJ," Lucy rounded the truck. "Thanks for fetching our horses."

"You're welcome. I hear last night was a blowout."

"You could say that. Did Izzy tell you she aced the apple bobbing at the shower?"

"She did."

"I knew she would. We used to play it at Halloween parties and she'd always win."

"I credit my good teeth."

He laughed. "You do have very nice teeth."

"I should. My father's a dentist."

He gazed at her. "Interesting. Didn't know that."

"There's a lot we don't know about each other."

"Yes, ma'am and that'll be the fun of it. Discovering new things every day."

Every day. But they only had two left. He couldn't be talking about this visit, so he had to be projecting into a shared future… in Seattle.

She'd better figure out what the heck she wanted to happen before he took the decision right out of her hands.

_28_

Inviting Izzy to hang out at the bunkhouse had been a spur-of-the-moment idea, and so far, it was going well. Millie usually came over with Jake on Friday nights and found something to do while CJ helped Jake with food prep. The kitchen only accommodated two cooks.

Millie had taken a notion to pick wildflowers tonight and use Mason jars to display them on the long picnic table out by the fire pit. No sooner had she announced her intentions than Izzy volunteered to help and off they went, joking around as if they'd been friends for years.

He and Jake had made chuck wagon stew so many times they worked on autopilot. While Jake handled cubing and browning the meat, CJ sliced and diced the veggies.

Jake presided over two skillets since they were making a double batch. "Hard to believe you got that phone call from Isabel last Friday while we were doing this exact same thing."

"No kidding." CJ washed the veggies and pulled his favorite knife out of the wooden block on the counter.

"Haven't had a chance to ask how last night went."

"Damn, that's right. I've talked to so many people today I forgot you weren't one of them. That's what you get for taking the day off to work on your cabin."

"Need to finish the porch so Millie can hang paper lanterns on it. She's fixated on having pretty lights on that porch."

"It'll look good."

"It will, but she wants bright colors and the whole idea was making the cabin nearly invisible to the naked eye. That'll nullify the program."

"Do you have another fight brewing about that?"

"No, we do not. I'm giving in on the lanterns. She's wanted some ever since Henri put them up in her yard. Millie loves embellishments. And I love Millie, so there you go."

"You're an inspiration to us all, bro."

Jake chuckled. "Glad to be of service." He tossed meat in each skillet and the cubes began to sizzle. "What came out of last night, anyway? Must be good. You're generally cheerful, but tonight you're optimism on steroids."

"I told her I love her and she said she loves me back."

"Just like that? No conditions on her part?"

"Oh, she has conditions. She started right in on her favorite theme—that loving someone means you make sure the situation is right for each of you."

"She's still against you relocating."

"She was then, but I swear I'm making progress. She didn't bring it up again. Instead we...well, you know."

"Uh-huh. Is that particular activity dazzling enough to change her mind about Seattle?"

"I'm doing my best. The rose petals helped."

"Yeah? Maybe I need to reconsider my stance regarding roses and petals."

"All I can say is that last night was great. But time will tell."

"You have precious little of it left, my friend."

"I'm aware. But I've leaped the biggest hurdle. She loves me and is willing to say so. I can't imagine living without her, now. If she gets to the point where she can't imagine living without me, game over."

"I hope tonight doesn't put a hitch in your giddy-up, cowboy. Chuck wagon stew night's all about the family ties Isabel's opposed to cutting. Henri's even decided to come."

"She has? Matt said the Babes were up to all hours."

"They were, but Henri's taken a nap since then. I assume she wants to observe you and Isabel at close range. A lot is at stake."

"That's true, but all along she's been preparing us to thrive anywhere. If I make this Seattle move work, she and Charley get most of the credit."

"Guess so."

"You don't think she'll be happy about that?"

Jake paused to glare at him. "Happy for you? Hell, yes. But happy that you're gone? No! Nobody wants to see you leave, bro." He cleared his throat. "Especially me."

CJ chopped some more veggies without saying anything. Moving ten hours away would cause his brothers pain and he'd failed to acknowledge that. Instead he'd focused on his own issues.

He took a shaky breath. "I wish there was a way for me to be with Izzy without putting everyone through this. But as I see it, this is the only viable option."

"Then you have to do it." Jake's voice was gruff. "We might not like the way the situation turns out, but we're behind you a hundred and fifty percent. And we—"

The kitchen door opened. "The wildflowers on the table make the place look like a trendy restaurant." Millie walked in followed by Izzy. "Whoa! You two must be solving the world's problems."

Jake flashed her a smile. "Somebody had to, and who better than me and CJ?"

"That's a scary thought. Hey, which one of you wants to donate your hat so I can teach Isabel the card flipping game?"

"You can use mine." CJ sliced a carrot and added it to the bowl of veggies. "It's hanging over my bunk." He paused to give Izzy a smile and treat himself to a glimpse of her. A purple tank top and snug jeans showcased the curves he'd be loving tonight.

She smiled back. "I got a demonstration of card flipping last night but there wasn't time to teach me."

"We'll be in the bunkroom if you need us," Millie said. "We'll just sit on your bunk, CJ, if that's okay."

"Sure."

After they left the kitchen, Jake lowered his voice. "She seems to like it here. Maybe that means you two will be able to visit often." He smiled. "Or you three, eventually."

"I'd like that."

"We would, too."

"By the way, have you ever heard of a game where you try to find safety pins in a bowl of rice?"

"Nope. Why?"

"They played it at the shower last night, and for some reason they want the Brotherhood to keep the bag of rice with the pins in it. Izzy gave it to me when I picked her up just now."

"Keep it where?" Jake scooped the meat into the stewpot and added the veggies.

"I don't know. I just tucked it into the drawer under my bunk for now." He rinsed off the cutting board and dried his hands. He was done until it was time to make the Texas toast. "Evidently they think we have a hidey-hole where we stash Brotherhood-related stuff."

"Why would they think that?" Jake added tomato sauce to the pot and pulled his favorite spices out of a drawer.

"I guess because they put Babes-related stuff in that big old safe of Henri's."

"They do?"

"That's what Izzy said."

"News to me." Jake turned the heat on low and covered the pot. "Hey, Millie! What's this about the Babes keeping memorabilia in Henri's safe?"

She came to the doorway. "I thought I told you about that."

He checked the pot and turned toward her. "Not that I remember."

"They use her antique safe for keeping what they jointly own, like the autographed Tim McGraw hat."

"The Tim McGraw hat." CJ smiled. "They were so excited about that concert."

"Yeah, the hat's special," Jake said, "but hanging onto a plastic bag full of rice makes no sense. Eventually it'll get weevils in it."

Izzy came in holding his hat and a deck of cards. "I think they just want to keep it pristine until the grudge match next week."

CJ looked at Jake. "A grudge match sounds like what they'd do, but why can't one of them hang onto the bag? No reason for us to be involved."

"The way of the Babes is mysterious." Jake shrugged. "They want us to keep it, so we'll keep it."

Izzy glanced at CJ. "Where is it?"

"Right now it's in the drawer under my bunk."

"I guess that's okay," Millie said. "But I thought the Brotherhood would have a special place in the bunkhouse for all your Brotherhood stuff."

Jake looked puzzled. "Like what?"

"Souvenirs, photo albums, sentimental things you can't replace."

"We don't have souvenirs and photo albums."

"What about things related to your oath?"

"It's all up here." Jake tapped his head. "Now I'm curious about this rice game, though."

"I'll fetch it." CJ slipped past Izzy and breathed in her scent in the process. Got slightly high doing that. Being in love was awesome.

When he returned, Izzy stood at the end of the kitchen table with her back to him while she flipped cards toward his hat sitting in the middle. She got one in and Millie gave her a thumbs-up.

"Good job, Iz."

She glanced over her shoulder. "Thanks. I have a long way to go before I'm in Millie's league."

"Don't we all." Jake stood watching, arms folded. He glanced toward CJ. "So that's what all the hoopla is about."

"Yep." He handed it over.

Jake tilted it back and forth. "I see little glints of metal. How many pins are in there?"

"Twenty," Millie said.

"What's the object of the game?"

Izzy paused and turned. "You pour everything into a mixing bowl and without looking, you feel around in the rice until you find a pin."

Jake's eyebrows lifted. "That's it?"

"That's it." Izzy went back to flipping cards.

"Sounds like a piece of cake. I wouldn't mind trying that. How about you, CJ?"

"Suits me. We could play tonight after dinner."

"Yes, we certainly could." He gave a nod of approval. "Something different."

"We'd have to ask, first," Millie said. "The bag is the official property of the Babes."

"Then we'll check with Henri when she gets here." Jake set the bag on the kitchen counter.

"Good idea. I think the guys will enjoy it, don't you, Isabel?"

"Definitely. Great game. Everyone should try it."

She and Millie were up to something, which tickled CJ to no end. Jake's comment today at lunch had been right on. Izzy was one of them, now.

29

Isabel's cheeks hurt from laughing. The men of the Brotherhood were in rare form tonight, teasing each other unmercifully all through dinner.

Their rowdiness was partly fueled by bottles of cider and a warm summer night, but clearly they were used to giving each other a hard time no matter what the circumstances.

They hadn't let go like this during the wedding, maybe because the occasion was life-changing for one of their own. Evidently chuck wagon stew night was all about fun.

And what could be a better after-dinner event for slightly toasted and unsuspecting cowboys than the rice and safety pin game? When Henri granted their request to play it, she insisted they should go first to show the ladies how it was done.

Everyone got up from the long picnic table and gathered on chummy stumps around the fire pit. They didn't need a fire for heat, but Rafe had made a small one so the smoke would keep away mosquitoes.

An over-confident and clueless CJ volunteered to start the game. Tucking the bowl between his knees, he flexed his fingers. "Come to poppa, tiny safety pins." He nodded to Lucy, the timekeeper, closed his eyes and buried both hands in the bowl. He kept his jaunty attitude through two failed attempts.

Then he plunged in for the critical third try. "Got one!" Bits of rice clung to his fingers, but no pin. "*Sh*...ucks! Shucky darn!"

Isabel laughed. "Shucky darn?"

He glanced at her. "When we play a game with ladies present, swearing is frowned upon."

"Can the ladies swear if they want?"

"I asked that when I was a first timer," Kate said. "You can, but you'll feel like a potty mouth when they're coming out with *tarnation* and *dagnabbit.*"

"I love *dagnabbit.*" Rafe grinned. "That's your all-purpose swear word, right there."

"You'd better polish it up and have it ready, bro." CJ handed him the bowl. "I predict you're gonna need it."

"Naw. I'm good with my hands. Everybody says so." Rafe positioned the bowl, nodded to Lucy and shoved his fingers into the rice. Three minutes later, he was pin-less. He glared at the bowl. "*Dagnabbit!*"

CJ chuckled and stood. "This activity calls for some musical embellishment." He sauntered over to his guitar leaning against the picnic table. Propping his boot on the bench and balancing the guitar on his thigh, he launched into the chorus of *Another One Bites the Dust.*

"That works!" Rafe left his seat, grabbed a stick of kindling and joined CJ, pounding out the rhythm on the table.

CJ exuded raw energy as he belted out the lyrics. Isabel had experienced that level of intensity in him once before, when she'd asked for it... in bed. Her breath stalled.

They ended the chorus with a rock-star flourish and exchanged a high five. He glanced at her and winked, his smile sexy as hell. Her body clenched in response and she shivered.

"You won't need that number for me, losers." Nick puffed out his chest. "Better dust off *We Are the Champions.*" He took the bowl, settled it between his knees and rubbed his hands together. "Behold the power of friction!"

The power of friction didn't help Nick. Laughing, he picked up a piece of kindling and joined CJ and Rafe for another chorus. Leo did no better. When Garrett lost, he went to the table, flipped the empty stewpot upside down and drummed on it during the increasingly raucous song.

By the time Matt joined the men at the table, the noise was deafening. Isabel stood to get a better view as the guys busted moves and yelled out the lyrics with no attempt to stay in tune.

Millie laughed. "They've officially lost it."

"Brought to their knees by pins and rice." Kate exchanged a grin with Henri.

"Sounds like they're gonna sing it all the way through." Henri glanced at Isabel. "They're not always like this."

"Yes, they are," Lucy said. "Just not quite so ramped up. The game tipped them over the edge."

"Obviously." Isabel returned her attention to the guys as they ended the song, sent up a rowdy cheer and toasted each other with cider.

Nick handed CJ a bottle still dripping from sitting in the washtub of melting ice. He took it with a grin and laughed at something Matt said. Nick clapped him on the shoulder and Rafe playfully tugged his hat over his eyes.

Nudging it back in place, he looked beyond the circle of his brothers until his gaze met hers. He mouthed *I love you* and lifted the bottle in her direction. Then he gulped down most of the cider as sweat glistened on the tanned column of his throat.

"You look a little shell-shocked."

Lucy's voice pulled her out of her dazed focus on CJ. She turned and took a quick breath. "When you said CJ usually played his guitar on Friday nights, I thought he'd be doing ballads and stuff."

"Sometimes he does. Depends on the mood. I guess tonight called for some craziness. You okay?"

"Sure." Nope. But she'd needed to see this.

* * *

"Okay, what's up?" CJ glanced at her as he drove back to her cabin.

"What do you mean?" Stupid question, but maybe she could delay the conversation.

"You were having a great time until you weren't. I figure it had something to do with me playing *Another One Bites the Dust.*"

"I loved the entire episode. And your brothers are hysterical."

"But you've been sad ever since."

"What makes you say that? I've—"

"Yeah, you've been cheerful and smiling, talking with everyone like nothing's wrong. Doesn't fool me a bit. What's the problem?"

She clenched her hands in her lap. She was better off not looking at him so she stared out the open window into the darkness. The crickets were loud tonight. "Same old problem. There's no way this will work out for us."

He groaned. "Jake was right."

"About what?"

"He was worried that you'd see me with the gang and conclude I'm too deeply rooted to make the transition."

"Because you *are* deeply rooted."

"Of course I am. Henri and Charley were experts at tilling the soil. But I'm stronger than you give me credit for, Izzy. Let me prove it to—"

"I can't take that chance. You have everything you love here. You'll have none of that in—"

"I'll have *you.* And Cleo Marie. That outweighs all the rest."

"That's never been tested. You have no basis—"

"I have tested it!"

"How?"

"In my head. I've mentally put myself in your apartment."

"You've never seen it."

"Doesn't matter. I'm in a generic apartment. No Henri, no Brotherhood, no Buckskin Ranch. Just you." He pulled up in front of her cabin and shut off the motor. "Imagining the joy of sharing your space..." He unfastened his seatbelt and turned to her, his gaze intense. "I want that. I want it so bad I can taste it."

Tension made her clumsy and she fumbled with her seatbelt. At last she unlatched it and faced him. *Breathe, girl.* "Living together would be exciting...for a while."

"If you think I'll get tired of you—"

"Not my point. You'll start to miss the people you're used to seeing every day. And the longer you go without—"

"We'll talk on the phone. Hell, we can video chat on the phone."

"It's not the same."

"I know." His chest heaved and he stared out through the windshield as if gathering his forces. "Bottom line—I'll do whatever it takes so that I can hold you every night." He turned back to her. "Look me in the eye and tell me you don't want me there."

She took a deep breath and met his steady gaze. "I don't want you there."

"You're lying, Iz. You want me right this minute. Just like I want you. We love each other. You can't deny—""

"I'm trying to stop you from making the worst mistake of your life!"

"You can't know that."

"Yes, I can!"

"Izzy, you're just plain scared. I don't blame you, but—"

"You should be, too!"

"Let's go inside." He reached for the door handle. "We'll talk. Iron this—"

"Talking isn't going to solve anything."

He smiled. "Then we'll have to try something else."

Panic squeezed the air from her lungs. "Don't come in." She knew the truth. But the fire of his lovemaking would incinerate it. She opened her door and started to get out.

He grabbed her arm. "Don't do this."

"I have to." She glanced over her shoulder and sucked in a breath. The agony in his gray eyes ripped her to shreds. "Let me go."

"*I love you*. You said if I ever saw you heading for a cliff, I should—"

"This isn't a cliff." Her voice shook. "It's a fork in the road. Let me go. And don't follow me."

His grip loosened. "Izzy…" He'd never said her name like that, like he was drowning. "This isn't over."

She pulled her arm free and used the door to steady herself as she climbed down. Her legs were wobbly. No, it wasn't over. It would never be over. They were having a baby.

30

Izzy hadn't managed to close the truck's door all the way. CJ took it as her subconscious balking at what she'd done. Dragging air into his tight chest, he focused on the cabin and willed her to come back out.

Damn it, why did Jake have to be right? This shouldn't be happening. She loved him. They belonged together. He'd contacted every riding stable in the Seattle area and received encouraging text messages from two of them. He'd planned to tell her tonight.

While everyone had been busy serving themselves stew, he'd pulled Henri aside and asked to meet with her during his lunch hour tomorrow. He'd written up a formal resignation to give her even though she might not require one. Putting it on paper would let her know he was serious and she needed to start looking for his replacement.

Although proposing to Izzy tomorrow night would be awesome, he didn't have a ring and shopping for one required driving into Great Falls. No time. Seattle would have a bigger selection, anyway, so he'd given up on getting engaged before she left.

But now... was there anything he could do to turn this around?

He stared at the cabin door and the light shining from the front window. If her light was still on, there was hope. *Come out, Iz. Please. Tell me you had a moment of insanity. Say you just realized you can't live without me.*

The light in the window went out. He'd seen movies where the hero pounded on his sweetheart's door until she opened it and let him kiss her. If he could just kiss Izzy, everything would go back to the way it had been before.

But what worked well in the movies wasn't a great idea in this case. The guests sleeping in nearby cabins wouldn't appreciate a scene like that. Worse yet, he wasn't entirely confident she'd open that door no matter how hard he pounded on it.

How could he convince her that the move to Seattle would be good for him, for her, and Cleo Marie? As he sat in the darkness listening to the crickets, nothing brilliant came to him. Okay, this was depressing. And unmanly.

Reaching across the passenger seat, he opened the door slightly and gave it a good tug so it closed tight. Then he started the engine and left his seatbelt off as he drove to the bunkhouse. Living dangerously.

Laughter and rowdy conversation drifted out the screen door as he approached. Matt and Lucy had left the picnic area when he and Izzy had taken off. Jake and Millie had been saying their goodbyes, too, along with Henri.

Sounded like a poker game was in progress with the guys who still lived in the bunkhouse—Nick, Garrett, Rafe and Leo. They might have invited Kate to play since she loved the game.

Sure enough, the leaf had been removed from the kitchen table to create a manageable size for poker. The five of them were well into a game, but the action came to a screeching halt when he walked into the kitchen.

Kate was the first to speak. "*Now* what?"

He'd rehearsed his explanation on the way over so he could say it without choking up like a loser. "After watching me having a great time with you jokers, she's concluded I'll ruin my life by moving to Seattle." He crossed to the fridge and took out a bottle of cider.

"She's been saying that all along." Rafe folded his cards and laid them on the table. "What's different?"

"This time she took a stand, wouldn't let me through the door." Still hurt like hell. He twisted the top off and took a soothing gulp of the cool liquid.

Nick shook his head. "That's harsh, bro."

No kidding. "Jake predicted this could happen, but by the time he warned me it was too late to change the plan." Pulling out a chair, he took a seat at the table.

"That's it, then?" Garrett frowned. "You're giving up?"

"Hell, no, I'm not giving up." He held tight to the bottle and put his other hand under the table so nobody would notice he was shaky. "But I'm not sure what my next move should be."

"We can brainstorm while we play." Leo's suggestion was casually made, but his gaze was far from casual. He was worried.

Wouldn't be helpful to focus on Leo's concern right now, so he looked away. "Perfect." He took another swallow from the bottle. Good thing they'd stocked up recently. "Deal me in."

* * *

He didn't remember setting his alarm, but evidently he had. Loudest alarm ever. He shut it off, sat up slowly and swung his legs over the edge of the bunk. Today would be no fun. No fun at all.

Somebody had made coffee. He'd go get some. In a minute. First he had to make sure his head wouldn't explode if he attempted to stand.

"Here, bro." A hand appeared with a couple of aspirin in the palm.

He squinted up at Nick. "Thanks." He managed to pick up the tablets, get them in his dry mouth and swallow some of the water from the glass Nick offered him. "Never been that drunk."

"But you sang on pitch. That was—"

"I *sang*?"

"You sang." Rafe approached with a steaming cup of coffee. "We didn't know you'd learned that one."

He sighed and scrubbed a hand over his face. "She's *My Kind of Rain*?"

"That one," Nick said. "You do a nice job with it. Not as good as Tim McGraw, but close."

He thanked Rafe for the coffee and inhaled the smell of it. "Can't believe I sang it."

"Several times." Rafe sounded amused.

"Aw, geez. Was Kate still here?" He sipped the coffee, careful not to burn his tongue. It already felt too big. If he scalded it, he might not be able to keep it from hanging out of his mouth like a happy St. Bernard.

"Kate left when the poker game broke up," Nick said. "You fetched your guitar after that."

"Glad she was gone, at least." He drank more coffee. The jackhammer in his head gradually became more like the soft thud of hooves on a dirt path. The guys looked less blurry, too. "Did we brainstorm an Izzy plan?"

Rafe nodded. "We all agree you should sing her that song. You told us it's your couple song." He grinned. "You told us that a lot."

"Look, I'm not standing outside her window like some loser and—"

"No, that would be lame," Nick said. "You'll perform it in the gazebo during the celebration tonight. I don't know which song you'd picked, but do this one, instead."

"I'm scheduled to play?" The jackhammer returned.

"That's what Henri said last night. You don't remember?"

"Not really. It's possible I agreed to play weeks ago when they were rounding up entertainment. I have a vague memory of it." Everything was vague, now. Exactly what he'd been going for as he'd downed copious amounts of cider.

"Check with Henri," Rafe said. "She has a copy of the program."

"I have a meeting with her at noon for something else." He'd spaced the reason. It would come to him once the fog cleared. "I'll ask her then."

"Good. Let us know when you'll be performing and we'll make sure Isabel's in the vicinity. Sing straight to her." Rafe smiled. "She'll love it. Guaranteed."

"Not convinced of that, but it's something, anyway. One thing's for sure. I've already logged in rehearsal time on that number."

Nick laughed. "That you have, bro."

"Thanks for putting up with me, guys." He glanced toward the bunkhouse window where the sky was growing lighter by the second. "Are Leo and Garrett gone already?"

"They are," Nick said. "They had a sunrise ride going out."

"For some unknown reason I remember that. And I kept them up late. Nice."

"They're okay. Better off than you."

"No doubt. I need to get dressed."

"I can cover for you," Nick said.

"Yeah, me and Nick were gonna let you sleep but then your alarm went off."

CJ craned his neck and peered up at Rafe. It was like standing at the base of the flagpole on the square and gazing at the Stars and Stripes rippling overhead. "You're so damn tall."

"Genetics."

"Your parents were tall?"

He shrugged. "Guess so. Don't know for sure."

"Sorry. You mentioned that once. I'm not myself this—"

"Forget it. Listen, you could use a couple more hours of shuteye."

"You stayed up as late as I did."

"True," Nick said. "But we didn't try to suck up every bottle of cider in the house. Rafe and me, we've got this."

"Nope. Thank you kindly, but I'll do it." He set the mug on the floor, clenched his jaw and stood. The jackhammer tortured him while he searched in vain for his shaving kit. Where the hell was it? Oh, yeah. In Izzy's bathroom.

He didn't have time to retrieve it now, so he'd go unshaven to the barn and maybe to the meeting with Henri. Getting his razor back would be a hassle. He hit the showers and the hot spray revived him considerably.

The morning went fast, thank God, and he had only five minutes to spare when he parked in front of Henri's for their noon meeting. He glanced at her rose bushes before climbing the steps to her front porch. Eons had passed since he'd picked roses and gathered petals for Izzy.

Henri was at the screen door before he had a chance to knock. "The word's out, son." She pushed open the screen and beckoned him inside.

"That I spent the night drunk and singing a Tim McGraw song over and over?"

"That, too." Her smile was kind. "You had your reasons."

"Does Izzy know I did that?" He took off his hat.

"Maybe not. Lucy's the only one who might tell her. I'm guessing the information went to Matt and no further."

"I'd prefer she didn't find out." He rubbed his chin. "Pardon the scruff, but my shaving kit's in her cabin and I—"

"Never mind. Makes you look rugged."

"Especially with my bloodshot eyes."

She gazed at him. "Charley showed up at my door once looking the way you do. We'd had a nasty fight and I'd...well, he thought I was through with him."

"Why? What did you say?"

"That our relationship was never going to work."

He winced. "Did you mean it?"

"At the time. I had some rigid thinking going on. But I never wanted to put him through that again. We were married within a month."

"If only I could be so lucky. I scheduled this meeting to turn in my resignation, but I didn't bring it, after all."

"Come on into the kitchen. I fixed us each a sandwich."

"Henri, you didn't have to—"

"It's not often I get to have lunch with one of my boys. If there's a chance you'll be moving on this year, spending time with you is even more precious. I opened a couple of virgin ciders since we're still on the clock."

"Yeah, I may never drink again." He followed her into her sunny kitchen. "I love this room." In the early days, they'd had many talks here—Henri alone or Henri and Charley, a double dose of parental wisdom.

"It's my favorite room in the house." She waved him over to a round table that looked out on the backyard. The places were set and the food and drink waiting. "Have a seat."

He laughed. "Still testing me, are you?" He walked to her side and pulled out her chair. "If you please, ma'am."

She winked at him and slid onto the chair. "Well done. I've been told these gestures are old-fashioned, but Charley believed in them, too. When you boys carry on the tradition, it's like I still have a little bit of him with me."

"I can't think of a better reason to keep it up." He scooted her in and took the chair opposite her.

She put her napkin in her lap. "You were going to hand in your resignation. Does that mean you started job-hunting in Seattle?"

"Yes, ma'am." He settled into the familiar routine of eating a meal with Henri. Cloth napkin in his lap, he waited for her to start. "Got a couple of good responses."

"What's your plan, now?" She picked up her sandwich.

"That depends." He'd skipped breakfast and he was starving. But he managed to keep from wolfing down the sandwich.

"On what?"

"Whether Rafe and Nick are right that I'm on the musical program tonight."

She blinked. "You definitely are. Didn't you hear me say that last night?"

"Sorry. I was...my mind was on other things."

"You're still doing it, I hope."

"Yes, ma'am. In fact, it might be my last chance to change Izzy's mind."

31

What a horrible night. Groggy and disoriented, Isabel dragged herself out of bed when light sifted through the break in the curtains. She slipped into the white terry guest robe she'd grown to love and ground beans for coffee. After brewing a cup in her French press, she padded barefoot out to the porch, leaving the door open so she'd hear her phone.

Sitting in one of the Adirondack chairs didn't provide the relaxation she craved. Instead she paced the cool porch floor and paused along the way to sip her coffee.

Tire tracks in the dirt parking area in front of her cabin could be from any number of trucks that had pulled in here this week. But some were from CJ's. She'd finally figured out last night that he wouldn't leave until she'd doused the lights.

When she couldn't hear the rumble of the engine anymore, she'd walked out to the porch and let the evening breeze dry her cheeks. No telling how long she'd stayed out there listening to the crickets.

Not just crickets, either. A couple of owls had carried on a back-and-forth and she'd swear a wolf had howled in the distance.

She'd fought the urge to go down the steps and walk the grounds, but she hadn't gathered enough knowledge about this unfamiliar land to walk alone at night with confidence.

Lucy had. She'd acclimated beautifully to the ranch and its wonders. The cabin she and Matt were building would be a remote haven for her artist's soul. She'd told thrilling stories about coming across bears, bobcats, and a slow-moving porcupine during her rambles.

CJ must have encountered his share of critters, too. She'd never asked about it, but he must have stories as fascinating as Lucy's. He might not have volunteered the information because it was second nature to him. He clearly had no idea how perfectly he blended into his environment.

Her phone chimed with Naomi's ring. Good time to check on her big sister—before the shop opened and after the sexy cowboy had left for work.

Pain radiated through her. He'd be on the job by now, partnering with one or two members of the Brotherhood, maybe getting some comfort and advice while they shared the morning's tasks.

She stepped inside and picked up her phone from the table by the window. "Hi, sis."

"Hi, yourself! So far your flight time hasn't changed. I have the shop covered so I can pick you up. Can't wait to see you!"

"Same here, squirt."

"You haven't called me that in years."

"I haven't?"

"No, and your voice sounds weird. Have you been crying?"

"Not recently."

"What's wrong?"

She sighed. "I don't think there's enough time to—"

"Talk fast. It's CJ, isn't it?"

"He got this dumb idea he should move to Seattle, but—"

"*Move here*?" Her voice squeaked.

"I can't let him. This is where he belongs, where he shines. If he relocated, he'd lose...his CJ-ness. He wouldn't be the same person. He wouldn't be the guy I fell in love with. He—"

"Iz, you're sobbing."

"No, I'm not!" She fumbled in the pocket of her robe. No tissue. She used the sash to mop her eyes. Blowing her nose on it would be gross, though.

"You're crying your eyes out because you're hopelessly in love with your child's father. That's wonderful and horrible at the same time."

"I know! Hang on. I need a tissue."

"Oh, I'm hanging on. What are you going to do?"

"Get a tissue." She plucked several from the box in the bathroom and blew her nose one-handed.

"I meant about CJ."

"Nothing. I'm flying out of here tomorrow and I'll keep all our communications about the baby short and impersonal from now on."

"That's bullshit, sis."

"I have no choice. He can't live with me in Seattle. He's determined and optimistic about doing it, but...I can't bear to watch him become...someone who's not CJ."

"So part of what you love about him is the cowboy vibe?"

"Yes! Because that's who he is to the bone. He was born to ride a horse, and oh, how he loves working with those animals. His second home is the barn and oh, yeah, he plays a mean guitar. He gets to do that all the time around here. In Seattle, he'd—"

"You're crying again."

"Just a little." She wadded up the soaked tissue and shoved it in her pocket. "Anyway, that's the gist."

"Izzy, you do have a choice."

"If you're going to tell me to take a chance and invite him to live with me, I'm not—"

"You could move there."

She gasped. "Are you *crazy*?"

"Sometimes, but I—"

"What about Cup of Cheer? What about you? Moving here would mean selling the shop, and I could never—"

"I don't want you to sell it, either. I love working here. In fact, I love running the place. So, open another one in Apple Grove and let me run this one. Nobody said you can only have one—"

"You really *are* crazy!" Her heart raced. "Do you know what that would entail?"

"Yes, I do, and I'll bet the second one will be easier to get going than the first. Any bank will be happy to give you a loan because you've proven you can successfully operate a business in a highly competitive market."

"They won't if it's not a viable concept in this location. I appreciate the thought, but Apple Grove is a little town. I doubt I'd get the traffic to support—"

"At least promise me you'll think about it. Or better yet, research it. You're good at that."

"So are you." She took a shaky breath. "But that brings up the other point. I'd be ten hours away from you. And Mom and Dad. And the only place I've ever called home."

"Have you been happy with CJ at the Buckskin this week? And don't lie, because I know you have."

"Of course I have."

"And has he indicated he'd do whatever it takes to make this work between the two of you?"

"Yes."

"Then let him put all that energy into making it work for you in Apple Grove. You'll be so busy with him, the baby, and the new business you won't have time to miss us."

"That's really crazy."

"Yeah, okay, maybe that's over the top. But you could visit a lot. In fact, it'd be a tax-deductible expense!"

That made her laugh. But not for long. "What if it doesn't work out?"

"What if it does? You could have it all, Iz. You just have to be open-minded. Listen, I gotta run. Think about what I said. I'll see you soon. Love you."

"Love you, too." She disconnected, but stood staring at the phone for a long time.

The image Naomi had painted hovered like a mirage in front of her eyes. She didn't want to leave her family, move to Montana, and build another coffee shop from scratch.

Did she?

* * *

Apple Grove's Founders Day celebration was in full swing as Isabel and Kate joined the folks strolling the square. The streets had been blocked off to become pedestrian walkways and fairy lights sparkled in the trees.

"Thanks for rescuing me from an awkward situation." The knot in Isabel's chest loosened. She'd ridden in with Matt and a very nervous Lucy, who was getting her first lesson in pulling a horse trailer with her new truck.

They'd parked next to a riding arena that was within walking distance of town. While the Brotherhood and the Babes organized the barrel racing demonstration scheduled soon, she'd had nothing to do but avoid CJ.

Kate smiled. "Happy to. I'm not much help to them, anyway. Last year I wandered over here by myself while they were setting up. It's nice to have a buddy this year."

"How many of these have you been to?"

"This'll be my third and I'm still dazzled by it. Those fiddlers were here last year. One guy does an amazing job on *Orange Blossom Special*."

Isabel glanced at the gazebo, which was also decorated with fairy lights. CJ would be performing a number at some point.

She'd meant to check for a program online, but her focus today had been area demographics and commercial rental property. Oh, who was she kidding? She'd avoided looking up the time. Any reference to CJ made her stomach churn.

She took a deep breath. "When's CJ playing?"

"Nine-thirty." Kate looked at her. "Did you ask so you could be there or so you could head off somewhere else?"

"I haven't decided." She sighed. "I'm a hot mess, Kate. I may watch from a distance, so he can't see me. I might throw him off his game."

"I have it on good authority that he'd like you to be there. Where he can see you and vice-versa."

The knot in her chest returned. "Does he still think he can change my mind?"

"Of course. He's CJ."

"Of course." She swallowed.

Kate put her arm around her and gave her a quick sideways hug. "I hate that this is so tough for both of you."

"Thanks, Kate."

"Hey, the shops are open. We could pop into one of them or browse the crafts fair." She gestured toward the tents and booths set up on the lawn surrounding the gazebo.

"Just walking the square helps the most." Soon they'd pass the vacant shop on the corner, the only one for rent on the square.

"Then we'll do that."

When they reached it, she paused. "What used to be in there?"

"A yarn shop. You know the little knitted baby caps Red and Peggy gave you on Thursday?"

"Yes. They're adorable."

"Red and Peggy bought the yarn from Thea. They're very sad she left town."

"For lack of customers?"

"Oh, no. The shop was always busy. She just got tired of the snow in the winter. She's only been gone a couple of weeks. It's a good spot. Somebody will be in there soon."

"I'm sure. With display windows on the front and the side it's a tasty piece of rental property." Plenty of room for booths with a view of the square.

Kate laughed. "I suppose you'd look at it from a businesswoman's point of view. I just loved the feel of the place. I bought yarn even when I don't knit or crochet, just because I loved going in there."

"Why?"

"It's cozy and yet you're part of things since you can look out on the square." Kate's phone pinged. "That's my alarm. We need to get back."

"Okay." She took one last look at the corner shop. Perfect location.

But would she be any happier here than CJ would be in Seattle? Her hormones said yes, but her brain wasn't convinced.

If she took the leap and lived to regret it, she could turn a difficult situation into an unbearable one.

32

Izzy was avoiding him. That hurt, but CJ wasn't about to chase after her. The bleachers were crowded for tonight's event. Nice to see that so many folks wanted to see the Babes do their thing.

Garrett, Nick and Leo had claimed a spot along the top row and they waved him up. He made the climb and took a seat next to Garrett without checking to see where Izzy had parked herself. When he made a quick survey, he found her three rows down and about ten feet to his left sitting with Kate and Rafe.

Nick must have caught him looking. "Have you talked to her at all?"

"Nope."

"Her choice or yours?"

"Hers. I've caught her eye a few times but she just turns and goes in a different direction."

"That sucks."

"Yep."

Garrett glanced at him. "I'm sorry, buddy. I thought for sure... well, never mind."

"Yeah, I thought so, too." He focused on the seven women mounted and waiting near the arena. A large suede-cloth banner hung on the fence with *Babes on Buckskins* stitched in elegant gold letters. "I'm happy for the large turnout."

"Me, too," Garrett said. "Are they any good?"

Nick laughed. "Clearly we've neglected your education."

"Was that the wrong question?"

"Let me put it this way," CJ said. "Ed is one of the top barrel riders in the country and she's been teaching the others in her private indoor arena for... how long has it been, guys?"

"Years," Leo said.

Garrett's eyes widened. "Ed's still competing?"

"And winning." CJ shifted his position so he could keep track of Izzy from the corner of his eye. "She picked up another trophy last month, which is even more impressive since she was on a relatively inexperienced horse."

"That's amazing for someone her age."

"Better not reference her age when you're talking with her, dude," Nick said. "She's liable to challenge you to an arm-wrestling match."

"Thanks for the tip." His gaze shifted to the arena. "Looks like they're ready to start. I was interested before. Now I'm excited."

"They're fun to watch." And a welcome distraction. CJ let himself go, cheering and whistling after each run.

Izzy got into the spirit of the occasion, too, leaping up and clapping wildly for each of the Babes. She went especially crazy when Lucy took her turn on Muffin. Ed's seasoned gelding gave Lucy an edge and she was clearly thrilled about it.

His phone pinged as the demonstration ended. Izzy? Heart racing, he checked the message. Rafe.

Nick leaned around Garrett. "What's up?"

"Rafe's confirming he and Kate will make sure Izzy's there for my song."

"Good."

"I'd better grab my guitar and hotfoot it over there. Not a lot of spare time."

Nick raised his hand for a fist bump. "Go get her, bro."

"Thanks." His gut tightened. Most critical performance of his life.

* * *

The country band that was becoming a regular at the Choosy Moose was packing up as CJ approached the gazebo.

He mounted the steps. "Forgot you guys had the slot in front of me."

"Yep." The lead singer glanced up and shoved back his hat. "You're a solo act?"

"Yeah. I'm not a pro like you guys, but the organizers thought I should do a song, so here I am."

"Which song?"

"*She's My Kind of Rain.*"

The guy squinted at him. "I thought I recognized you. You're the dude who requested that tune on Tuesday night for a special lady."

"I am."

"So now you're singing it to her on your own?"

"Something like that. Hoping it helps my cause."

"Usually does." He turned toward his bandmates, who were disconnecting the speakers. "Hey, hold up a minute." He swung back around to face CJ. "How'd you like the guys to give you some backup? Obviously, they know this one."

"I appreciate the offer, but—"

"I'm sure you'd do great on your own, but take it from me, it's nice having more instruments in the mix. Makes for a richer experience." He smiled. "Go big or go home, dude."

CJ laughed. "You have a point. This is my Hail Mary pass. I could use the help."

"Excellent. I'll announce it for you, too. What's your name?"

"CJ Andrews."

"I'm Drake Cutler. Let me introduce you around, CJ."

By the time he'd met the band members, established the key and tuned his guitar, it was time.

Izzy was out there, standing with Kate and Rafe about five or six yards from the gazebo. The rest of the Buckskin gang was arranged around them in a loose semi-circle. They likely wouldn't stop her if she tried to bolt, but the configuration made him smile.

Drake did a bang-up job introducing him and the song, making him sound like a local celebrity.

As the band played the intro, CJ focused on Izzy, stepped up to the mic and began to sing. Onlookers wandered over and the crowd grew, some inching closer to the gazebo, but he could see over them. His vision narrowed until there was only Isabel Marie Ricchetti, the mother of their child, his soul mate, his kind of rain.

Then...magic. Izzy walked slowly toward him, slipping through the crowd until she stood directly in front of him, tears streaming down her cheeks. She stood very still, her gaze locked with his. And those beautiful brown eyes told him all he needed to know.

How he finished the song was a mystery. He must have, because generous applause crashed around him. He lifted the strap over his head and leaned the guitar against the gazebo railing as he descended the steps and gathered Izzy into his arms.

He kissed her salty lips and she hugged him so tight he couldn't breathe. He didn't care if he passed out. He didn't care about a damned thing except this moment when the woman he loved was squeezing him as if she'd never let go.

He could kiss her forever, but the muted voices of the many people surrounding them finally convinced him to lift his head and murmur the first words of his new and vastly improved life. "We should probably move."

Her smile trembled. "Where would you like to go?"

"Anywhere you go."

"What if I stay here?"

"In front of the gazebo?"

She shook her head. "In Apple Grove."

"I don't get it." He didn't care if he did or not. She could talk all the nonsense she wanted when she looked at him with stars in her eyes.

"I'm leaving Naomi in charge of the shop and coming to live here. I—"

"Wait!" Panic gripped him. "You can't leave your shop! You've given your life's blood to it. If you abandon it to be with me you'll—"

She placed a finger over his mouth. "I'm not abandoning my shop. I'm putting Naomi in charge of it and opening a second one here. Expanding my business. Naomi suggested it and at first I thought she was crazy but—"

"She is crazy. Your home is in Seattle."

"My home is with you."

"But—"

"I may not love this town and the ranch as much as you do, but I have a feeling it won't be long before I do. And I know I love you and the person you are when you're surrounded by the people who love you, too. I want more of that. Lots more of that. I also want a home in the woods with my cowboy and my baby. When I open a coffee shop on the square, I'll have it all."

"You're making my head spin."

"What about your heart? How's it doing?"

He took a shaky breath. "It's full of love, but my head is...I'm having a tough time believing that—"

"Believe it, Cornelius Jasper Andrews. We're going to live happily ever after in Apple Grove—me, you and Cleo Marie."

He choked up. No words existed for the incredible joy she'd just given him. "Izzy..."

"I'm here." Cupping his face in both hands, she rose on tiptoe and kissed him softly. "You're my kind of rain."

* * * * *

When bachelor cowboy Nick La Grande
volunteered to stand on the auction block to
raise money for Raptors Rise, he never
expected the winning bidder to be hairstylist
Eva Kilpatrick. But she has a definite plan for
putting all his rippling muscles to good use in
TRUE-BLUE COWBOY, book four in the
Buckskin Brotherhood series!

* * * * *

New York Times bestselling author Vicki Lewis Thompson's love affair with cowboys started with the Lone Ranger, continued through Maverick, and took a turn south of the border with Zorro. She views cowboys as the Western version of knights in shining armor, rugged men who value honor, honesty and hard work. Fortunately for her, she lives in the Arizona desert, where broad-shouldered, lean-hipped cowboys abound. Blessed with such an abundance of inspiration, she only hopes that she can do them justice.

For more information about this prolific author, visit her website and sign up for her newsletter. She loves connecting with readers.

VickiLewisThompson.com